# Bloodrunner Bear

(Harper's Mountains, Book 2)

## T. S. JOYCE

# Bloodrunner Bear

ISBN-13: 978-1533245618
ISBN-10: 1533245614
Copyright © 2016, T. S. Joyce
First electronic publication: May 2016

T. S. Joyce
www. tsjoyce.com

NOTE FROM THE AUTHOR:

This book is a work of fiction. The names, characters, places, and incidents are products of the writer's imagination or have been used fictitiously and are not to be construed as real. Any resemblance to persons, living or dead, actual events, locale or organizations is entirely coincidental. The author does not have any control over and does not assume any responsibility for third-party websites or their content.

Published in the United States of America

First digital publication: May 2016
First print publication: May 2016

Editing: Corinne DeMaagd
Cover Photography: Furious Fotog
Cover Model: Tyler Halligan

# DEDICATION

For 1010.
It's probably strange to dedicate a book to a rickety old singlewide trailer, but my life completely turned around when I lived there. Not only that, but it became a character in these books—a pivotal part in all of Damon's Mountains, and now in Harper's Mountains. So cheers, 1010. You were full of spiders and mold, and keeping you from falling apart was a full-time job, but I've never loved a home more.

# ACKNOWLEDGMENTS

I couldn't write these books without my amazing team behind me. A huge thanks to Corinne DeMaagd, for helping me to polish my books, and for being an amazing and supportive friend. We've had a crazy adventure, haven't we, C? And to my husband, who is doing so much behind the scenes, and wanting no attention for it. He has always been there with me through my odd work hours, propping me up when I feel like I'm falling, and has the uncanny ability to understand when my characters are being unruly little beasties. Those are the days he has a stiff drink and a hug ready for me, and I wonder if he can actually read my mind. A huge thanks to Golden Czermak, for being such an incredible photog to work with, and to Tyler Halligan who is the perfect Aaron on this cover.

And last but never least, thank you to the crew, you, the reader, the reason I am able to do what I love. You let my books into your imaginations and for that, I can't tell you enough how much I appreciate you. Thank you for asking for each book in Damon's Mountains, and now for the books in Harper's Mountains. We are on this wild ride because of you.

# ONE

"Fire department, call out!" Aaron Keller yelled as he ducked under a thick plume of smoke and frantically searched the tile floor of a large bathroom. There was still one woman unaccounted for according to the landlord, and this place was going up in flames fast.

The roar of the fire was only eclipsed by Aaron's heavy breathing inside his mask. Flames licked at his turnout gear as he passed a coat closet that was actively burning. That could be trouble if this part of the wall collapsed when he was in the back of the small rental duplex.

"Aaron, fall back," Chief said from the safety of the street outside.

Aaron's partner, Mark, had been over the radio, updating the boss man on how bad it was in here and how much time they had left, because yeah, after a while firefighters got an instinct for that. They understood the behavior of fire on an intimate level. Aaron knew Chief was right, but he had one more room, and he'd be damned if a woman burned because he left too early. Not today. Losing people stuck with his inner bear. He was supposed to protect people, not let them die.

"Fire department, call out!" Aaron yelled louder as he shoved the final bedroom door open with his shoulder. The back of the room was a solid wall of yellow flames, roiling like waves up toward the ceiling, the fire searching for air, seeking oxygen. With the closed windows in here, there wasn't much left.

There she was. A woman in a robe lay on the floor, motionless. Shit.

Mark was yelling into the radio for him to evacuate, his voice too damn loud for Aaron's oversensitive ears. Ignoring his partner, he bolted for the woman. The ceiling was coming down, and while he had fire resistant clothing and shifter healing, if this woman was still alive, she wouldn't survive a cave-in. Aaron skidded on his knees and threw himself on top of her.

The roar of the rafters hitting the floor around them was overwhelming, and something heavy struck him on the back. The pain was instant—too much weight, too much pressure—but Mark was right there, pulling away debris. Aaron could tell from the heat easing off his body. The instant he was able, Aaron sat back on his knees, yanking the woman with him, and then he and Mark bolted out of the blazing inferno. The ambulance was just pulling up, but the firefighters were trained paramedics, and Aaron knew what to do in the moments before the team reached them on the sidewalk out front. He set the woman down, stripped off his mask and gloves, and felt for a pulse. It was there, but faint. He put his cheek in front of her face but couldn't feel a breath. He tilted her head back, plugged her nose, and prepared to do mouth-to-mouth resuscitation but Aric dropped down beside him, shoving him out of the way. "Back off, shithead. You'll kill her."

Kill her? Who had just pulled her out of the burning house? Fuckin' vampire. Aaron hated Aric, but there wasn't room for a brawl right here in the dark street as they lost this lady to smoke inhalation.

Aaron paced, a snarl in his throat as his instincts to protect her from Aric warred with his need to help with the hoses.

"Aaron, do work," Chief demanded.

Chest heaving, he kept his eyes averted and nodded. His eyes would be bright green-gold right now, and Chief always told him and Aric to keep their "supernatural shit" to themselves. A month working for the Bryson City Fire Department, and Aaron was pretty sure Chief would never accept the bear side of him. It wasn't like in his last firehouse in Breckenridge. There, half the crew had been bear shifters, and no one cared about him exposing his inner animal. They were accepting, but here, everything was different. He still felt off-balance.

Aric pushed the heel of his palm against her chest one last time, then stopped and set his ear over her mouth as if checking for breath. His lips moved like he was mumbling something, but Aric's sandy brown hair had fallen in front of his face, covering his murmured words. The woman gasped for breath and coughed over and over. And though he might hate Aric for what he was, for the scars Aaron now bore on his neck, and for what his coven had tried to do to his alpha, he couldn't deny the fact that Aric was good at raising humans from near death.

Aric slid an oxygen mask over her face, and the paramedics scattered toward a pair of coughing teens on their hands and knees in the yard of the connected house.

"Aaron!" Aric barked out, his eyes full of horror.

"What?"

"My baby," the woman choked out through the mask, her eyes vacant. "Where's my baby?"

Fuck! Aaron pulled on his mask and sprinted for the open doorway. The fire hadn't reached the front of the house yet. A nursery. He must've missed a nursery.

"Aaron, I said fall back!" Chief yelled over the radio. "Get your ass outside now! That's an order. Fuck. Mark! Bring him back!"

Living room, kitchen, two bedrooms, two bathrooms, no nursery. The ceiling was raining burning sheetrock and embers. The smoke was too thick near the bedrooms. Maybe the baby had been sleeping in the woman's room? Why the fuck didn't she have the baby in her arms?

Hose water blasted through the living room window onto the flames against the back wall, and Aaron covered his mask from the spray. He had to keep a good visual, and the smoke was already making it hard. There was no crying.

*Please be okay. Please be where I can reach you.*

In the hallway, the rafters caved, and burning debris landed hard on his forearm, yanking him down. His arm was pinned under him, against the searing materials. So hot. Burning. Franticly, Aaron yanked his arm out from under the rubble and backed away. The way to the bedroom was blocked now. *The baby.*

A rough hand grabbed his turnout gear and pulled him backward. Mark. "There's no one left!" he yelled through the radio. "You'll get yourself killed for nothing!"

Aaron shoved off him. "There's a baby!"

Through his mask, Mark's eyes were scared as he looked up at the wall of flames above them. The human had a family—a wife and two kids. He was young, three years out of Fire Academy. He was a good one. Mark wouldn't leave without him, and now it was the baby or Mark. Aaron's heartbeat was roaring in his ears as he tossed one last glance back to the bedroom. He could just make out the walls coming down, and he knew it was too late.

He grabbed Mark's shoulder, and together they ran from the house. Now, he was going to have to break it to the woman that he'd failed her. He'd done this before, told families about their loved ones he hadn't been strong enough, or fast enough, to save. This was his least favorite part of the job. She would look up at him, her eyes hollow, because deep down she would already know he hadn't pulled off a miracle. Even though he didn't have her baby in his arms, she would still ask him, and his answer would destroy her entire world. And he would carry that burden, along with all the others, until the day he drew his last breath.

But when he saw the woman, she was smiling and looked relieved. What the hell? Maybe she was in shock. He cast Mark a quick glance to make sure he was out safe with him. His partner was talking low to Chief. Aaron made his way through the paramedics and approached the woman slowly.

"Thank you for saving me," she said, her voice scratchy from the smoke.

"But...your baby. I couldn't get to it."

A frown of utter confusion commandeered her face. With a slight shake of her head, she whispered, "I don't have baby."

"But...you said..."

Horror washed over Aaron as his arm began throbbing in rhythm to his pounding pulse. He looked down at his searing arm. The fire had eaten through his jacket, and he could make out the angry red blisters of his ruined skin beneath. In a moment of clarity, the memory of Aric's whispers while resuscitating the woman flashed through his mind. It wasn't some incantation he'd been uttering to keep her from death, but mind-manipulation.

Aaron pulled off his mask. Fuck his gold eyes and who saw them. He blinked slowly and raised his furious gaze to Aric who was on the hose with a couple of the others from their station. Aric was watching him. A predatory smile spread across his face as his eyes turned black as coal. Fuckin' vampire.

Rage pulsed in Aaron's veins before he charged

him. He was to Aric in a moment, pummeling him, his fist shattering against the asshole's stony jaw, but Aaron didn't care. "You could've gotten me killed!"

Stupid fucking smile on Aric's face. "That was the point, Bloodrunner."

"Aaron, stop it!" Chief yelled from behind.

They were trying to pull him off the vamp, but Aaron wouldn't be moved. He was searching the ground around them for something wooden, something he could shove through Aric's chest cavity and kill him with. This was too much, too much for his inner monster to let pass.

*"Kill her."*

"What?" Aaron shook his head. That sounded like his bear. Kill her? Kill who?

*"Kill the dragon. Kill, kill, kill. Kill your unworthy alpha. Kill the dragon."*

Aaron shook his head hard. *Stop it, Bear.*

*"Kill the Bloodrunner Dragon so you can become alpha."*

It was Aric. Aric was manipulating his animal. Aaron slammed the King of the Asheville Coven against the concrete, and there it was, the first crack in Aric's poker face. He winced in pain, so Aaron

11

slammed him against the driveway over and over, a snarl in his chest. His arm hurt so fucking bad, but he would break his own bones to kill this asshole for what he'd done. For what he was suggesting.

Aaron loved Harper. She was his cousin. She was good. Maybe she was the best person he'd ever known. The best alpha. Good, good, good.

Aaron opened his mouth and roared his fury.

He would stake Aric a thousand times before he would hurt a hair on the Bloodrunner Dragon's head.

# TWO

*1. Nice*

*2. Polite to wait staff/big tipper*

*3. Independent/has a job*

*4. ~~Big dick~~ Medium dick is fine*

*5. Good teeth/Good smile*

*6. No tattoo/piercings*

*7. Enjoys the outdoors*

*8. Doesn't snore*

*9. Likes to snuggle*

*10. Protective but not controlling*

*11. Good listener*

*12. Not dramatic/argumentative*

*13. Sexually attractive*

*14. Not a shifter*

Alana Warren sighed and narrowed her eyes at the list she and her sister had come up with their freshmen year in college. The page was worn, tattered really, and had permanent fold lines. The edges had disintegrated, and there was a coffee stain that had smeared a couple of the numbers on the list. She needed to let up on her expectations because she'd come to realize no one fit what her twin sister had deemed a "dream man." By some miracle, it had worked for Lissa, and she'd found Todd. Well, it had worked as far as Alana knew. She had no clue about his medium to large dick, barf. But the magic of the list had apparently run out, because Alana had never found her someone-special by it.

The bell to her coffee shop and bakery dinged, and she looked up with the plastered smile on her face that she always had for customers. It was the ass-crack of dawn, and usually it was just her regular seniors in this early. Through the wall of windows up front, dawn had barely broken the horizon with pretty grays and soft pinks, but the view was completely blotted out by the giant man who meandered in.

She blinked slowly as she dragged her gaze from

his thick-soled boots to his navy pants and matching shirt. There was a fire department logo on the man's mesmerizing chest. She could make out his puckered nipples on account of his muscles pressing enticingly against the thin fabric. Decorating the curves of his strong arms, tattoos peeked out from under his short sleeves. When Alana's attention landed on his throat, she froze. It was scarred on one side, from the neck of his shirt to just under his ear.

"How can I do you?" she asked, eyes riveted on his mangled throat.

"What?" he asked, a hard edge to his tone.

Oh, God. "Uh, I mean, how can I help you? I mixed that up with 'what can I do for you' and made it into 'how can I do you.' Which…" She shook her head and forced a laugh. "That's not what I meant. I'm good on the…doing it…area…of my life." *Shut the fuck up!*

The giant snorted, and it was then she dared a look into his eyes. Bright blue under blond eyebrows and sparking with curiosity, though the set of his mouth was grim.

He locked his arms on the counter and lifted his attention to the chalkboard menu above her.

"Oh, my gosh. Your arm!" She jammed a finger at

the long burn mark that had eaten into his flesh. It was red and blistered, but he didn't seem to be favoring it. "Do you want me to call an ambulance?" She jerked her cell phone from her pocket and hit the 911 before he reached over her and poked the *end call* button.

"I know the guys in the ambulance. I already told them I was fine." He arched his animated brows. "And I am."

"But it looks like you stuck your arm in an oven. Doesn't it hurt?"

"Nah. It's a reminder."

"Of what? Not to cook your arm?"

"To be more careful with who I trust."

Mysterious, yummy. Alana fought the urge to add that to the bottom of the list and instead carefully asked, "What can I get you?" Besides her teats and treasure box because he could have those free of charge.

"Uh, I've never been here before."

Obviously. She would've remembered a sexy yeti like him.

"What's good?" he asked.

"Everything." She gestured grandly to the

breakfast pastry window beside her. "I bake everything myself. And the coffee doesn't suck either."

"Try her raspberry cinnamon rolls," Bradford called out from the table in the corner. He and his buddies always came in first thing to talk about the latest news in town—which wasn't that enthralling because Bryson City was population 1500. Nothing exciting ever happened here.

Sexy Yeti tossed old man Bradford a look over his shoulder, nodded a greeting, then told Alana, "Yeah, that sounds good. And a coffee. Black."

"Manly," she muttered, entering his order into the cash register.

Sexy Yeti was in the middle of pulling his wallet from his back pocket and asked, "What's that?"

"Hmmm?" she asked.

He was pointing at the dream man list, so she snatched it off the counter. Heat blasted up her neck and landed in her cheeks. "N-nothing."

"A medium dick, huh?"

Crap. Her fingers shook as she reached for a to-go cup. "What name should I put on this?" She hovered her sharpie over the cardboard sleeve on the cup.

"Pen."

"What?"

"People call me Pen One Five."

"Why not Pen Fifteen?"

Pen shrugged and looked at the total on the screen, slid the money across the counter, and gave her a half smile. "I'm lookin' forward to that pastry."

Okay then. She wrote *Pen15* on the cup and internally kicked herself. She had definitely made a play to get Sexy Yeti's real name, and he'd refused it. He strode toward a booth on the opposite side of Bradford and the Senior Seven, as they called themselves.

She'd never seen him around these parts before, and she knew almost everyone in town. It was a big deal when newcomers showed up, so no doubt he would have a dozen tits in his face by Friday from the eligible bachelorettes in this one-horse town.

That's why she was moving away from here. No future, no one to settle down with.

As her thoughts buzzed around the move preparations, Alana gathered his pastry into a small to-go box and poured his coffee. She looked at the name on the cup and called out, "Pen...is." She narrowed her eyes at the *Pen15,* which definitely looked like the word 'penis,' and snorted. Well-played, Sexy Yeti. "Penis," she muttered again louder with a glare for him. His face cracked into a grin. He definitely had good teeth and a good smile. Number five, check.

As he approached from his booth, he told her, "You should add great sense of humor to your fuck-list."

Her mouth fell open at his crassness. "It is *not* a fuck-list. This is what I want in a long term relationship, not a one-night-stand."

Unable to handle the look of at that awful burn on his arm a second longer, she pulled the first-aid kit out from under the counter and rifled through it. "And furthermore, I'm not like that. I don't just...you know...sleep with men and move on with my life the next day. Sex means something big to me." She slapped the small tube of burn cream onto the counter. Alana wanted to stay offended, but Sexy Yeti's face went completely slack as he stared down at the medicine. And when he looked back at her, his eyes looked strange. A different color almost. There was a moment of such raw vulnerability there, it made her feel off-balance. Alana rested her palms on the counter so she wouldn't sway on her feet.

"Ask him out!" Bradford demanded from where he sat with the Senior Seven.

"Bradford," Alana groused, "I told you a dozen times you can't take your teeth out and leave them on the table for the other customers to see!"

"I would say 'no,'" Sexy Yeti said.

His words stung, as if someone had spiked a volleyball directly into her face. In a whisper, she said, "I didn't ask, but why would you say no? Is it the way I look?" The scar always caught men off guard, and it sucked that it was hindering this one's opinion of her, too.

The man shook his head slowly, eyes locked on hers. And then he pointed to her list, to number fourteen. *Not a shifter.* Now his eyes were definitely a different color. More of a muddy greenish gold than blue, and he smelled different—like fur.

"Because," he murmured, "even if I was looking for a mate, which I'm not, we aren't compatible." Something unfathomable flashed through his eyes, and a soft growling sound emanated from him.

They both froze, locked in each other's gazes.

He blinked hard, his blond brows furrowing, and in a rush, he pulled something from his pocket and set it on the counter with a soft *click*. It was a rusty old paperclip. "Thanks for the medicine." He stuck the tube of burn cream into his back pocket, gathered his coffee and pastry, and left her café without a single look back.

She'd always found the *ding* of the bell above the door so pretty, but now it rang hollowly as the loneliest sound in the world.

# THREE

Aaron threw his leg over the seat of his bike and turned it on, revved the engine. His heartrate was pounding too fast, but why? And why the hell had he given that woman his lucky paperclip? Baffled, he cocked his head and watched her through the window of Alana's Coffee & Sweets. Her nametag had read *Alana*, so she must be the owner. The woman had piled her dark curls up on top of her head, but a few wisps had escaped, framing her heart-shaped face with pretty chestnut-brown highlights. She had curves for days, big tits, perfect ass, and that hourglass shape that drove his boner wild.

He'd been shocked when she'd asked if he didn't like the way she looked. Was she insane? She had dark, soft-looking skin his fingers had itched to touch. Her animated doe-brown eyes and dark lashes had made it hard for him to look anywhere else. Her lips were full and colored with a pretty, glossy pink, and her bright smile had rocked him to the core. It was a little crooked from some old injury she'd healed from. Yeah, she had a deep and obvious scar that ran from beneath her nose through the left side of her lip, but who the fuck was he to judge? He'd had his neck ripped out by Aric a couple months back. Alana had stared at the scars on his neck when he'd walked into her coffee shop, so she knew he bore old injuries, too.

That woman in there was the most striking human being he'd ever seen.

Aaron pulled the pastry from the box and shoved the entire raspberry roll into his mouth. He liked how direct she'd been with him, asking him straight out if her appearance bothered him. Hell no. He'd almost pointed to his inflated dick pressing against his pants as proof, but she didn't need to get attached, and neither did he.

He wasn't the mating kind, and that list she'd

written out said they weren't a match.

Aaron felt strange without his lucky paperclip in his pocket, but he didn't regret giving it to her. In fact, his bear was humming in satisfaction, which made no damned sense. He'd been so riled up after that fight with Aric, but one little conversation with Alana, and he was feeling calm again? Huh.

Aaron's arm hurt like hell, and for a moment, he considered using the burn cream Alana had given to him. But she'd swapped that for his paperclip and he wanted to keep it as his new lucky charm instead. She would probably throw away his paperclip, but he had to be okay with that. It was done.

Aaron took a long swig of the hot coffee, ignoring the burn.

He should tell her his name... No. Aaron shook his head and pulled his jacket on for the ride back to Harper's Mountains. He ran molten hot, but it was late November, and the Smoky Mountains where he'd recently moved got bitter cold sometimes, especially at the higher elevation.

He cast Alana one last glance as she refilled coffee cups for the seniors with a big smile on her lips. So fucking beautiful. He chugged the rest of the coffee and tossed the empty cup into the wastebasket next to his parking spot. Shaking his head hard to rid his bear of the instinct to go back in there, Aaron hit the throttle and blasted out onto Main Street. A selfish part of him hoped she heard the throaty rumble of his motorcycle and watched him leave, but for the life of him, he couldn't figure out why. He'd shut her down for a reason. His life was a freaking tornado right now.

A soft, easy-going woman like Alana would get eaten up by a man like him.

Giving her the paperclip had been okay, but he'd been right not to give her his name.

As he weaved his way on the back roads toward the mountain range on which the Bloodrunner Dragon had settled, dawn lit up the cloudy sky. He hadn't stopped in the coffee shop because he was hungry, but was stalling instead. Wyatt had been challenging him for Second in the Bloodrunner Crew. Not his fault—Wyatt's bear was a brawler like his was. But it didn't help anything if he came home riled up. It would set Wyatt off.

Before he'd talked to Alana, Aaron had felt like his skin belonged to Bear. He'd been searching desperately for something to calm his animal in the early morning hour right after he got off his shift, and the inviting glow of Alana's Coffee & Sweets had lit up the sleeping Main Street.

The sign was dilapidated and some of the lightbulbs behind the letters had burned out. Inside, the tile floors had been cracked, and the walls a bland shade of eggshell white. She'd hung colorful pictures on the walls, but not even those could distract from the water-damaged ceiling tiles near the door or the shoddy wainscoting that had been installed. She probably rented the building and wasn't allowed to make many changes. He could do a lot for the place.

Aaron shook his head hard again. *Stop it.* She didn't need his help to fix up her shop. That woman was perfectly capable of taking care of herself.

The café was right down the road from the station, and damn it all, as much as he wanted to convince himself she wasn't a big deal, he was already plotting ways to go back after every shift and fuel up on coffee and boners before his trip back to Harper's Mountains. Pathetic.

The coffee wasn't half bad, but it was Alana's animated eyes and crooked smile that had thoroughly distracted him from the verbal reaming he'd taken from Chief. "You can't kill your co-workers," and yada, yada. Aaron had stopped himself from staking Aric with the wooden handle of his ax, so really, Chief should be giving him a damn trophy for his self-control, not giving him a speech about how he'd hired Aaron because of his family name, and how he needed to live up to expectations. The Kellers were Fire Bears with a well-known honorable name in their Breckenridge community and around the world. They were the origin—the first to come out as shifters to the public over twenty-five years ago. For a long time, Aaron had been part of the chaos that surrounded those uncertain times, working in the same firehouse with his father, Cody Keller, and three uncles, Boone, Gage, and Dade. Aaron had lived in the shadow of his name, and apparently that shadow stretched all the way to Bryson City, North Carolina.

He didn't regret moving here to be a part of Harper's crew, but damn it was hard figuring out how he fit in.

Pulling through the gate of Harper's land gave him a warm sensation like it always did. No matter what was going on in the firehouse, this place felt like home. Maybe it was the people here, the Bloodrunner Crew he was a part of, or maybe it was the land itself. Maybe it was the first cabin he passed with the lopsided house number 1010 beside the door. Or maybe it was that he'd pledged his fealty to Harper Keller, one of the last Bloodrunner Dragons. The invisible thread that linked them had been pulled taut during his shift at the station, but it loosened as he made his way past 1010. He was bound to Harper now and always felt better around his alpha.

Farther up the dirt road on the right, there was a double cabin sharing a roof, but separated by a breezeway in the middle. Weston Novak and Ryder Croy were probably still asleep in their beds. Aaron drove slowly up to the last cabin, the smallest. His humble abode. His bear settled even more when he parked his bike next to his old truck under the metal awning he'd installed. On snow-days, he would have to give up his bike, but it wouldn't be as bad as in Breckenridge where snow reigned in the winter months.

He had two days to recover and find his center again before his next twenty-four-hour shift at the station, and he planned to use that time to work on his cabin. The old creaky shack had barely been livable when he'd moved in last month, and he needed to make it weatherproof for the oncoming winter.

The first thing he did was turn on the heat. His little two-bedroom house was just as cold inside as it was outside right now. Since his arm felt like he was holding a hot poker against it, Aaron pulled the giant first aid kit out from under the bathroom sink and rummaged around in it for some pain relief. Shifter healing was one of the perks of having the inner animal, but burns were rough. They were slower to heal and most of them scarred. Yet another mark from Aric. Someday, he was going to kill that mother fucker. He was biding his time now, sure, but someday, someway, he was going to drive wood through that vamp's chest cavity and piss on his ashes.

"Knock, knock," Harper said softly as she rapped her knuckles on his bathroom door.

He startled and let off a warning snarl. "Dammit, Harper, you can't just barge in here. What if I wasn't decent?"

"I've seen your dick every time you've shifted

since we were practically zygotes. Calm your balls, man." Her eyes, one brown, one blue with a long pupil, pooled with worry. "What happened?"

"I don't want to talk about it," he murmured, the same answer he always gave her. Talking about what happened on his fire shifts never made him feel better. The faster he pushed everything out of his mind, the better for Bear.

The long, low rumble of Harper's dragon vibrated the bathroom as he cleaned the wound under cold water. "I could order you," she ground out.

"But you wouldn't because you're better than that."

"Alphas make orders all the time, Aaron. Don't act like me caring is me being weak."

He inhaled, then blew out an irritated sound. "Aric has mind control abilities."

"What," Harper drawled out. "You're shitting me."

"I shit you not. He made a woman tell me her baby was still in a burning house, and then he was in my mind telling me…" He made a ticking sound behind his teeth and winced as he slathered his burn with medicine from the kit. "Forget it."

"Telling you what?" Harper lowered the lid on the toilet and took a seat on the porcelain thrown. His queen. "Tell me now, or I'll bug you all day."

"Don't you have better stuff to—"

"No, Aaron! I don't. My job comes second to you and the boys. It's different for me now, and I'm going through all these protective instincts I have no idea how to control, so spill it or I'll make it my mission to pry it from you."

"He was telling me to kill you."

Harper's mouth dropped open. "W-what?"

"Yeah. He can control what the animal inside of me says. In Bear's voice and everything. And for a second...for a second, it felt like a real good idea. He told me I should kill you and take alpha."

"Jesus."

"Jesus has nothing to do with Aric, Harper. Should I quit? He's been working night shifts at the station for years and has seniority. What do you want me to do?"

"Firefighting is your livelihood. If you give it up, what will you do?"

Flounder. Spiral. Lose his purpose. But Harper didn't need to know how much leaving his career would demolish him, so he shrugged and leaned against the counter, eyes passive like he didn't care either way.

Harper knew him, though, and her sense of awareness had heightened since she'd become alpha. She bit her bottom lip and then told him, "Don't quit. You aren't a runner, and Aric doesn't own Bryson City."

Aaron snorted. "Just Asheville."

"Bullshit," Harper said, looking none-too-impressed. "He is king of one coven of eight vamps, not a million. They're small-time. Find a way to work with him, Aaron. You need some kind of tentative alliance. Aric won't convince you to hurt me. He can't. You're stronger than him."

As she made her way to the door, Aaron hoped with everything he had that she was right, because hurting Harper would be like ripping his own heart out.

"Oh," she said, turning at the door. "Wyatt needs another fight."

Aaron groaned and rocked his head back. "He can have Second, Harper. I just got him back as a friend. I don't want us to keep bleeding each other."

"Look, I get it. I do. But this is how new crews work, and both of your bears need to establish a pecking order. Right now, you two are both dominant enough to run your own crews. You wanted under me, so this is the gig. You fight, you establish a Second, and then we move on." Her eyes softened as she leaned on the doorframe. "Look, Wyatt's bear is struggling. He's used to being alone, and his control is slipping. I really think it's because of the crew being unsettled still. It feels too chaotic for him. It's hard for me to watch him go through this."

"Because you love him?"

"Yeah. I love him more than anything. And I love you, you big dumb oaf, and I don't care who is my Second so long as it gets worked out, okay?"

As he'd been watching Harper and Wyatt for the last few weeks, something inside of him had been shifting. He'd never wanted anything serious with anyone, but maybe it wouldn't be so bad if a mate could help him feel settled, like Alana had done in her coffee shop.

Maybe a fight would distract him from the confusion surrounding the pretty woman with the crooked smile. "Fine," Aaron muttered to Harper. He tossed the unused bandages back into the first aid kit and pulled his shirt off as he followed his alpha outside because, apparently, he wasn't done fighting for the day.

Alana's kindness had been wasted on a beast. Aaron had felt the effects of her thoughtful burn cream gesture for less than an hour before Bear was ready to rip out of his skin and brawl again.

# FOUR

Alana marked out number fourteen on the dream man list. Pursing her lips in concentration, she carefully and completely blacked it out with a permanent marker, then folded the paper and tucked it in her back pocket.

Snatching the basket of pastries off the end of the counter, she strode for the door, turned the hands on her clock sign to say *be back in fifteen minutes*, and made her way into the crisp winter weather outside. A few stores down, she gave a friendly wave to Fiona Cooper and her daughter who were walking along the sidewalk across the street.

"Hey, Alana!" Fiona called. "How's business?"

"Just fine," she lied. Business had never boomed for the coffee shop. In fact, to rent the space and keep up with her bills, she was barely breaking even every month. She'd had all these ideas for her café. Pretty paint colors, a mural on the back wall, chandeliers instead of the crappy, rusty lighting fixtures her landlord insisted on keeping for sentimental reasons. She wanted wood flooring and better display cases for her pastries and an updated kitchen in the back, but all that took money. She'd emptied her savings on startup costs two years ago, and if she was perfectly honest, Alana was disappointed she hadn't made enough profit to fix it up yet. She'd had all these plans, all these to-do lists, but all those dreams had circled the toilet when she'd failed to make enough to keep the place afloat long-term. She loved the café. It had made her feel brave for starting a business, and her heart belonged in between those four walls. But now she felt like a huge failure that she hadn't been able to do more for her café. That was the pitfall of starting a niche business in a small town. Not enough customers to sustain shops like hers.

Her heels clacking on the concrete, Alana ducked

into the giant open garage door of the fire station. She'd never been in here before, but there were three men cleaning the bright red fire engine that shone in the hanger. And one of those men was none other than the Sexy Yeti she'd met the other day. She'd known he would be here since she'd watched the firehouse for the past three days, waiting for him to show up on his Harley. And this morning, her stalking had been rewarded with the deep rumble of his bike echoing off the early morning Main Street.

He looked up from where he was folding a hose, dropped his gaze back to his task at hand, then jerked his attention back to her. "What are you doing here?" he asked so loud, his question echoed off the towering garage space.

"I brought you and the boys a thank-you basket."

"Please tell me there are lemon bars," Mark Trainor said as he and Bryant swarmed her like hungry seagulls. She'd gone to high school with both of them.

"Of course there are lemon bars." She handed over the basket, but snatched a box out before the boys laid waste to all the sweets she'd made them.

"This one is for you," she said, holding it out to

Sexy Yeti.

He shifted his weight from side to side, like a starving animal that debated the trustworthiness of her offered beef jerky.

"She isn't going to bite you, Aaron," Mark griped at him.

"Aaron," she murmured, testing his name on her tongue.

Around a bite of lemon bar, Mark said, "Yeah, you're looking at *the* Aaron Keller of the Breck Crew."

"What?" she squawked, too loud. Her heart leapt into her throat. She eyed him and tried to match his face to the boy who had been all over the news when the bear shifters had first come out to the public. He'd been a little blond, wholesome, squeaky-voiced kid when his crew had first made national news. Now he was a tall, strapping, tatted-up beefcake on a Harley.

Aaron angled his face away, his eyes hardening. Clenching his jaw, he took the offered box from her palm and ripped the lid off. He stared at the frosted bear-shaped pastry inside. "What's this?"

"This is my apology. The list..." She pulled it out of her pocket and showed him where she'd marked off number fourteen. "My sister made this list when we were in college, and I just kind of adopted it. She dated a shifter her sophomore year, a wolf. He was awful so she added it to the list. I just didn't want you to think I was prejudiced against you." Really, she'd been nipples-deep in guilt for the past couple of nights.

"Hmm," he said, nonchalantly.

"Aaron Keller," she murmured in disbelief. "I had a poster of you on my wall when I was growing up."

His eyebrows lowered over those clear blue eyes of his. "Why?"

"Because you were just a little older than me when shifters came out. I remember where I was when I saw your uncle Change your aunt on television. I remember Cora Keller's documentary on the news, and you were in it. And over the years, I would catch glimpses of you in interviews and pictures. I kind of watched you grow up, and you were hitting the milestones I was about to hit. Middle school, high school, driving. You were so…" Cute. Her cheeks heated and she ducked her gaze. "Anyway, I just wanted to say I'm sorry."

"Just so you know, wolves are assholes. Shifters aren't all like that, though."

"I know." Well, now she did.

"I'm not looking for a mate."

Shocked, she jerked her gaze to his. "Okay. I'm not looking for...that...either. Not from you. I have a date tonight. And I'm moving out of state soon anyway. As soon as my lease is up on my café, I'm moving to Madison, Wisconsin. Or maybe Boulder, Colorado. I read this article on the top hundred places to live in the country right now, and those made top ten." She was rambling so she clacked her teeth closed and swallowed her urge to tell this man her whole life story. Aaron Keller. Didn't that beat all? Maybe she should get his autograph.

"I've been asking you out for two years," Bryant said, offended. "Who are you going on a date with?"

"Someone from Asheville. I met him online. He looks very charming in his profile picture, and we are probably going to get married and have a dozen babies," she teased.

"Wow, you're creepily optimistic," Aaron said, his eyes narrowed to blue little slits.

"There is nothing creepy about optimism."

"I still don't understand why you wouldn't go out with me," Bryant said through a baiting grin, like the brute had ever shown any interest before now.

Aaron snatched the list from her hand and pointed at number four. "She's not into extra small dicks."

Alana laughed and clapped her hand over her mouth.

"Aw, man that's messed up," Bryant said, shoving another lemon bar into his maw.

"Some girls like little penises, Bryant," Mark consoled him through a grin. "They think they're cute."

"Stop it," Bryant muttered.

"It's like a 'lil belly button."

Bryant snatched the entire basket from Mark's hands and told him to, "Fuck off."

"Come on, Alana," Aaron said, handing her back the list. "I'll give you a tour of the firehouse before you go."

Well, at least he wasn't kicking her out straight away. She followed him to an open door on the far wall of the garage.

"There's the turnout room where we store our gear. That's where we dress when the alarm sounds."

She peeked into the room, lined wall-to-wall

with helmets, yellow fire suits, and gear. "And you get into the firetruck fully dressed?"

"For the most part. We're usually still pulling on a few things while we're getting there."

When she turned around, she ran into the solid wall of his chest and bounced off. Damn, the man didn't even move, but he did reach out and steady her arms so fast he blurred.

"Whoo," she said on a breath, squeezing his biceps as if she needed to use them to steady herself. A smile cracked his face as she tried desperately to make her hands stop squeezing his muscles. She wanted to bite his rock-hard pec, too, but something in her said Aaron wouldn't enjoy that as much as she would. "You're like petting an ice sculpture. You must work out a lot."

Aaron took a step out of her reach and chuckled, ran his hand over his longer hair on top as though he was self-conscious. He'd gelled it back, but now it flopped in front of his face. Alana clasped her hands in front of her to stop from brushing it aside. If he knew how big a super-fan she had been growing up, he would run for the hills. Shifters had been the rock stars for the rebellious youth, and Aaron had been a major player in the shifters coming out. She still had his poster in a box somewhere.

"Why are you smiling like that?" he asked, his chin dipped to his chest.

As if this tatted-up bad boy was actually having a shy moment. Come on. This man had probably banged shifter groupies by the dozen. Whoa, she didn't like that thought at all.

The smile dipped from his lips, and he canted his head, looking more animal than man with the expression he gave. "Now you smell angry."

"Not angry."

"Lie."

She'd forgotten about that little gem. Shifters could hear lies, but not that it mattered. She was the worst fibber in the history of the universe. He needed no heightened senses to tell when she was being untruthful.

Pushing past him, she asked, "Do you sleep here?"

"Uuuh," he fumbled, following behind. "Yeah. I work a few twenty-four-hour shifts a week. More if they need the help. It's not a big firehouse, but we help all the areas around here, too, so we stay busy enough." Aaron jogged past her and held the door open and gestured her down a gray tile hallway. There was an office on the right where Fire Chief Janson was on the phone. He came into the café sometimes and was always nice to her. She smiled and waved, and he mouthed a greeting and waved back before he frowned at Aaron and went back to his phone call.

"He's not my biggest fan," Aaron said low as he pressed his fingertips on the small of her back, guiding her forward.

Her body was taken with a shiver that emanated from where he touched her all the way up into her shoulders. Embarrassed, she rushed her response. "Why not?"

"I'm the new guy on the truck, and I've been having trouble following orders."

"Well, why don't you just follow orders then?"

"It's complicated. Things are really different here than where I'm from."

Alana looked up at him and tucked one of her wayward curls behind her ear. "Do you miss home?"

Aaron opened his mouth, but closed it again. He looked troubled, scrubbed his hand down his jaw.

"This is home now. I'll get my footing soon."

And she'd seen it—the exact moment he closed down on her. Mysterious Aaron Keller, grown up so differently than how she'd imagined. He strode around her and sauntered off down the hall, leaving her to trail behind. His reaction hurt, but why should it? They were strangers, and he didn't want to share. It wasn't the end of the world, so why did him shutting down leave this sick, hollow feeling in her gut?

With a steadying sigh, she followed Aaron to a big room with cinderblock half-walls separating six beds, each made neatly. "This is where we sleep, showers are in through there." The kitchen and dining area were next. It smelled like spaghetti sauce. "We take turns cooking."

"You can cook?" she asked, pleasantly surprised.

Aaron huffed a laugh, and she was again stunned by his smile. "Yeah, I do all right. Maybe not as good as you, though," he said, lifting the box with the bear pastry.

Relieved that his cold moment had thawed, she giggled and adjusted her purse on her shoulder. "I can bake, but I can't cook a steak to save my life. My dad was always the one on the grill, and my sister and I always took care of desserts."

Aaron leaned against the wall near the kitchen. "What did your mom do?"

"Uhhh." Alana didn't really want to drag the conversation into personal territory in the station, but Aaron was staring at her, waiting. Alana puffed air out of her cheeks and then explained, "She passed away when I was really young. I don't remember her very well." Alana shrugged and stared at Aaron's shoes.

"What happened?"

"She was sick for a long time. It's okay. I mean, it was so long ago, and I've dealt with it. My dad was an amazing single parent. He remarried a few years back. My sister and I were in the wedding and everything. I get along real well with my stepmom. It's a little strange sharing my dad after so long having him to ourselves, but he's really happy. He devoted his whole life to me and Lissa, and now it's time for him to enjoy his life."

"I'm sure he enjoyed raising you and your sister."

"Yeah. It was hard for him on his own, though. He was lonely, and oh! My sister and I fought like cats and dogs when we were younger, and he always had to play referee. I'm glad he found his other half."

Aaron's eyes had darkened to that sky blue she'd first seen in her coffee shop. "Yeah. His other half. Speaking of, why are you dating some doucheface from Asheville if you're about to move?"

"He's not a doucheface, and I'm going out with him to see if he entices me to stay," she said primly. Alana offered Aaron a flirty smile and turned, swished her hips, and made her way back down the hall that led to the garage.

"Can I ask you a question?" Aaron said from behind her.

As if she would deny this fine man anything. She hesitated at the open garage door and nodded. "Okay."

"What did you do with the paperclip?"

The slow smile that stretched across her face felt good. Alana dug in her pocket and lifted the rusty old paperclip in the air for him to see. "I kept it, of course. It's my good luck charm."

The smile lines on Aaron's chiseled jaw deepened with his sexy grin. He crossed his arms over his chest, puffing up his bicep muscles, and rolled his eyes heavenward. He murmured, "I'm new to town…"

"Uh huh." She waited, excited about where this was going.

"And I don't know many people outside of my crew and the station…"

"Uh huuuh."

He looked endearing as fuck as he bit the side of his lip and dragged it out. "So maybe I'll stop by the coffee shop in the morning, and you can tell me how your date went with Doucheface."

"Oh, you want to be friends."

Aaron laughed and scanned the street, then leaned against the side of the garage and nodded. "Yeah, friends."

"I will be the best friend you ever had on one condition."

His eyes sparked like dancing blue flames as he lifted his gaze to hers. "Name it."

Through a teasing grin, she murmured, "Don't fall in love with me, Aaron Keller."

His face went slack, and then he swallowed hard, his Adam's apple dipping into his muscular neck. "I'll see you tomorrow morning."

Her bravado would only get her so far, and she would squeak an excited sound if she opened her mouth, so she offered him a small grin, turned, and made her way back toward the coffee shop. She forced herself not to look back. She would embarrass herself if she did.

Aaron Keller had just offered her friendship. *The* Aaron Keller. He was so different than she'd imagined as a little girl, but in a good way. In the type of way that gave her butterflies and made her feel like she was floating with each step she took on the cracked sidewalk.

When she reached her coffee shop, she couldn't help herself. She had to peek back. Craning her neck, she looked around the trash cans and parked cars, and he was there, leaning on the side of the fire station, arms crossed and eyes on her. With an excited yelp, she waved her fingertips quickly and escaped inside.

And as she pressed her back against the closed door, Alana was a hundred percent sure her heartrate would never settle down.

Hang her date tonight—tomorrow morning couldn't come fast enough.

# FIVE

Alana had been tricked. Or catfished? Trey Langford was nothing like she'd expected. Online, he'd been polite, respectful, and wore a business suit in a professional looking picture. She wasn't after a man's money since she was perfectly capable of taking care of her own finances, but she was tired of dating boys instead of men. This was the trouble with dating at thirty. The good ones seemed to be taken, and the ones left in the dating pool were still single for a reason. And that reason, she'd found out over the last couple of years, was usually that they had the maturity of adolescent squids.

Trey belched and continued on about himself.
"So then I decided I didn't want to work for the man,
you know? So I quit my job, bought my business, and
now I don't have to answer to anyone. I wake up
when I want, work when I want, take days off when I
want."

Alana swallowed the bite of thin-crust pepperoni
and mushroom pizza and feigned interest. "What do
you do for your business?"

"I restock vending machines. Sodas, snacks,
candy, you name it. There is a need out there, and I'm
filling it. Hospitals, bowling alleys, professional
buildings...are you going to finish that?" He pointed at
a slice of bread on her appetizer plate she'd taken one
bite of.

Alana tried to compose the disgust off her face
but probably failed. Not that Trey noticed. He barely
waited for her to nod her consent before he grabbed
her bread and dunked it into the olive oil, herb, and
vinegar mixture Dante's Traditional Pizza Pies was
known for.

From the cozy front patio of the restaurant,
Alana sighed and looked down the street at the fire
station for the tenth time since dinner had started. It

was lit by street lights, and one of the hangers was open. She could see the fire engine but hadn't caught a single glance of Aaron. She wished she was sitting with someone else at this cute little two-seater table under Dante's pergola. Someone blond, mysterious, and covered in tattoos. She'd been so excited about this date with Trey a few days ago, but after meeting Aaron, she'd been dreading it.

Trey followed her gaze down the street, and Alana reminded herself there was just a little while left, and then she could go home and forget about this awkward night. She needed to at least give this guy a chance and anchor herself in the moment.

"So what do you do?" he asked.

She opened her mouth to answer, but he cut her off.

"Because I have to tell you, if this goes any further, I'm not really for supporting a woman who wants to stay at home with my kids. You'll have to take care of them and work. And I mean you need to be bringing in a big income. I'm not into gold-diggers. I make good money, and I don't want you thinking that's all I'm about. I need a teammate. I have financial goals I want to reach and can't do that on one income. I'm looking at early retirement, and if you think about it, settling down would put me even farther behind because we have to come up with retirement for both of us. Fifty-fifty sounds fair. Like tonight, I'm fine with paying for my meal, but you should have some pride and pay for your own."

Alana clenched her hands on her lap and barely resisted kicking his shin under the table. What a disgusting little troll. "I'd actually prefer to pay for the entire meal, Trey." She lifted her finger toward the waitress for the check.

"Really? In that case, I'm getting two desserts."

Alana unexpectedly giggled. She composed her face, but it fell apart again when she laughed louder. She started laughing so hard she covered her face. When she finally settled, she peeked through her spread fingers.

Trey was all mussed brown hair, dopey eyes, and a slight grin like he thought she was laughing at something funny he had said. "What?"

Alana gestured to Trey and shook her head. "It's just...you! Trey, you can pay for your own desserts. Fifty-fifty and all. Is this really what you talk about on first dates? Finances? You called me a gold digger! Sir,

I own my own business and don't need your money. I accepted your offer of a date because you seemed nice when we talked online and on the phone. But it's clear as crystal we aren't compatible. I wish you huge luck finding a woman to put up with"—she circled her finger at him—"all of that." She thanked Belinda for the check the waitress slipped onto the table, tipped her twenty-five percent, then slid into her cardigan and shouldered her purse. "It was nice to meet you, Trey."

"Well it wasn't nice to meet you. Your loss!" Trey yelled as she made her way down the sidewalk. "Good luck finding someone to accept all of *you*. Your scar looks hideous!"

What an asshole. The humor fell from her face as all her old securities came flooding back. She wrapped her arms around her middle to keep from falling apart. *Don't let him get to you like that.* She was stronger now. She loved herself. It had been a long road getting here, and Trey the Troll was not going to make her backpedal. Someone was out there who would accept all of her. He had to be. She believed there was a person out there for her, just like Lissa had found Todd and her dad had found her stepmom.

It just hadn't happened for her yet, but it would. Someday.

Stupid Trey for bringing up her scar. It was a low blow meant to hurt her. And it had. Her eyes burned with tears, but she blinked hard and kept them at bay because he wasn't worth the emotional effort. Determined to avoid the fire station, she stayed on the opposite side of the street as she headed back to the coffee shop, or more specifically to her small one-bedroom apartment at the back of the building where she could regroup and again convince herself the scar didn't matter.

"Hey!" Aaron's voice echoed down the street, and Alana jumped.

Quick as a flash of lightning, she dashed her fingertips under her eyes just to make sure she hadn't shed any of the moisture. "H-hey," she greeted him.

He stood inside the garage with a heavy-looking box balanced on the palm of his hand. His blond brows were furrowed with a frown. Aaron set down the box with a massive thud, then strode out of the station until only the two-lane street separated them. He dragged his gaze down her deep pink dress, fitted to her boobs and fuller from waist to hem. "You look pretty."

And then she lost it, eyes burning, lip trembling. Mortification swept over her. Her face fell, and she couldn't meet his gaze. Trey had been awful, and Aaron had just picked up all the pieces that were breaking apart and put them back together with those three words. You. Look. Pretty. Damn straight, and screw Trey for making her forget that for a moment.

She could hear Aaron's boots pounding on the pavement, and then he was there, hugging her shoulders. And holy mushrooms, he smelled divine. Masculine soap and body spray. Even his deodorant smelled good and, hell yeah, she was sniffing his armpit and crying and she would remember to be embarrassed in the morning when he wasn't hugging her and making her feel all warm and safe inside.

"The date?"

She nodded. "You called it. He was a total doucheface."

"Was he rude?"

Another nod.

A low, feral sound vibrated through Aaron's chest, and when she looked up, his eyes were on the man scarfing dessert at Dante's. "You want me to kill him?"

"Are you serious?"

Aaron's eyes locked with hers, and a tremor of terror zinged up her spine. They were so light, glowing almost, reflecting oddly like an animal in headlights.

"Yes or no?"

"No," she whispered through an accidental huff of laughter. "No, I don't want you to become a murderer because my date was an idiot." Her entire body was pressed against his, but she arched her neck all the way back to meet his eyes better. "You're really tall."

"Maybe you're just short," he said, the hint of a smile at the corners of his lips.

She giggled and sighed, thankful that Aaron had the ability to erase Trey with a little teasing.

Aaron rubbed her shoulders gently and cocked an eyebrow. "You're a very aggressive hugger, woman. I think you wrinkled my shirt."

"Passionate, not aggressive, and your shirt is weak if it is going to wrinkle so easily."

"I think you scratched me with your claws." Now

she could see the white of his straight teeth as he drew her hand up and studied her nails. She wouldn't admit it, but she'd told the woman who did her manicure today she wanted sparkly gold. It was the same shade as his eyes when he got riled up. She'd imagined those pretty gold-green eyes in a big brown bear, and secretly hoped she would get to see his inner animal someday.

"You'll heal." Alana wiggled her fingers at him. "Do you like them?"

Aaron smirked and dropped her hand. "Fishing for compliments so early in our friendship." He tsked and shook his head.

Alana pushed off him and laughed. "Don't make me fish then!"

"I like your nails, your hair, your make-up, your dress, and you smell like vanilla. You look sexy as hell, and if Doucheface let you go, it's on him."

And just like that, Aaron had her remembering her tough skin. "Yeah, fuck him."

"That's right." Aaron's smile stretched wider. He grabbed her hand as they took a few steps down the sidewalk, bumped her shoulder, and muttered, "Fuck him."

Alana stared down in shock at their intertwined fingers, his fair skin against her dark. There was something so beautiful about that connection. Aaron stopped walking and drew up in front of her. When she glanced up, he was staring at their hands, too, with such an intense look in his blazing gold eyes. His chest rose as he breathed in deeply, and when he lifted his attention to her face, he stopped on her lips.

Drawing closer to her, taking his time, Aaron cupped her neck with his giant hand and brushed his thumb gently over the scar on her lip, then across her cheek. A tender smile lifted and fell in an instant on his face.

Alana stood frozen, so hopeful that he would kiss her, but so scared because this thing growing between them felt huge now. It was one of those moments that had the potential to change her from the inside out. To make her look at the world differently.

How terrifying and exhilarating all at once.

Aaron leaned down slowly, and this was it. His lips were inches from hers, and Alana closed her eyes and leaned into him. And right as she could feel his body warmth seeping into her, a jarring alarm sounded.

Aaron tensed and jerked his attention to the firehouse as a woman's voice came over the intercom. "Truck forty-eight, ambulance forty-eight, automobile accident, possible fire, highway nineteen and eleven-sixty-eight."

Aaron pulled away and bolted for the flurry of chaos in the fire station. "I'll see you in the morning," he called over his shoulder.

Alana stood there stunned as she watched him disappear into the turnout room and then emerge with his crew, talking low and serious as they loaded up. The ambulance left the station just seconds before the fire engine blasted onto Main Street. Aaron was speaking into a radio from the front seat, but he locked eyes with her for a moment before he was gone.

A tsunami of worry washed through her middle. She'd never given a single thought to his job. Sure, she and her friends had joked about how hot firefighters were, but she'd never considered that someday she would have a stake in a firefighter's safety.

Up the road, the fire engine's blaring lights

disappeared, and Alana wrapped her thick wool cardigan more tightly around her shoulders to ward off the chill that had suddenly taken her body.

He would be fine. This was what he did, and he was a Keller. A bear shifter. He was good at his job and could survive a lot more than a normal human. So why couldn't she shake this sudden fear that had her paralyzed on the sidewalk of dark Main Street?

Caw!

Alana startled hard at the jarring cry of a bird and looked up at one of the trees along the street. A giant raven was bending a young branch under its weight and seemed to be looking right at her. Farther up the tree sat a snow-white owl, even more massive than the raven. Gooseflesh rose across her arms. Oh, hell no. She'd seen this movie before and was not about to get pecked to death.

Alana speed-walked down the street, daring a single look back at the strange birds in the tree before she escaped around her coffee shop and into her apartment.

Tonight had turned out weird. Disappointment over what a bulbous anal gland Trey had turned out to be, relief at Aaron's sweet compliments, safety in his embrace, the almost-kiss, and then the jarring alarm that had flattened her world in an instant. She was crushing hard on a man with a dangerous job. Alana was falling so hard, so fast, it left her unsteady. And now, as she stood in her living room thinking of the ominous birds in the tree, a trill of fear expanded in her chest. She got this strange sensation of being a rock, tumbling down a mountainside, faster and faster, and soon nothing would be able to stop her from hitting the bottom.

What was she doing?

She'd planned to move away from here and start over. To get out from under the shadow of her twin sister and find her own sense of self. But with every second she spent with Aaron, he put all of her plans in jeopardy and tempted her to grow her roots deeper into this little town.

He made her feel differently, but she couldn't figure out if that was a good thing or a very bad thing. In just three brief meetings with him, Aaron already wielded the power to make her reconsider her future.

Falling for a dangerous man like him was terrifying for a safe person like her.

# SIX

Deep inside of Aaron, the snarl of his grizzly was constant. A man had fallen asleep at the wheel and crashed into a ditch. The civilian who had made the call to 911 had pulled him and the man's six-year-old niece from the old SUV before it went up in flames. The man didn't make it. What kind of idiot didn't wear a seatbelt? Aaron was pissed. The entire thing could've been avoided if he wasn't toting his niece around late at night and had strapped the damn belt over his lap. It took one second to do and could've saved his life. It could've saved that little girl from going through all of this. She would be scarred inside for the rest of her life because she was the survivor. Watching her uncle die would be a part of her story.

Aaron had held the girl, Annie, while Aric worked to save her uncle with a couple of paramedics. Annie had cried against Aaron's shoulder until her mom drove up, frantic and sobbing. And all the while, the fire engulfed the car in the background while Bryant and Mark worked to put it out.

He was supposed to save people.

Aaron shook his head hard at the memory of Aric's grim expression as he radioed in to request permission to call time of death on the scene.

The girl would have some bruising from her five-point harness car seat but would be fine physically. At least her uncle had strapped her in, or tonight could've gone much worse. And thank God for the man who happened to pass the wreck and pulled her out before the fire caught in the engine. The what-if's piled up too high, and Aaron buried his face in his hands and squeezed his eyes closed. These shifts were the worst, when someone didn't make it. These were the ones where Bear felt out of control.

He grunted at the pain of his animal trying to claw his way out of Aaron's skin. He had to get out of the station before Chief saw him lose it. At least Aric wasn't around. He only worked night hours, on account of being undead and all. He would've slit his throat from behind if Aaron ever offered him a vulnerable position like this with the back of his neck exposed. By now, Aric was long asleep in whatever dark crevice he lived in.

Aaron glared at the sunrise through the back window behind him and sighed. Stalling wasn't going to help anything. His animal would be a monster all day until he could force last night from his mind.

Throwing the strap of his duffel bag over his shoulder, Aaron smoothed the bedding from where he'd sat and made his way out of the station with nothing more than a nod of the head for the guys on the new shift.

Outside, he revved the engine of his Harley and blasted down Main Street. He shouldn't stop at Alana's. He'd told her he would, but he wasn't safe to be around right now. He wasn't stable, and everything in him balked at the idea of letting Alana see him teetering on the edge like this. She would see how messed up he was and pull away.

Things had gotten about ten times more

complicated between him and Alana after their almost-kiss last night. He'd been serious when he'd told her he wasn't looking for a mate. She was human and fragile, and he saw loss of life on a weekly basis. He'd also seen what happened when a shifter lost a mate. Most of them never recovered. Hell, most of them had to be put down when the insanity took their animals. If he was this riled up over the lost life of a stranger, he would be a brute about Alana being safe. He would never want her to drive, turn on the stove, swim, or take any risk that could somehow result in her getting hurt. And what kind of life was that for her? No life at all. She was strong and independent and deserved a man who wouldn't stifle her. Aaron's protective instincts weren't an excuse to drag her down with him.

But...

He couldn't just pass her coffee shop and break his word.

At the last second, Aaron pulled into the small parking lot, shoved the kickstand down, and cut the engine. She was inside serving coffee to a family of four, her face transforming into that beautiful crooked smile. She said something and laughed, and he couldn't just barge in there and ruin her day with his moody bear.

He growled and scratched his head in irritation. He couldn't figure out how his dad and uncles had done it. They'd been firefighters for years, and he'd never seen a single crack in their hard exteriors. They just managed.

He crossed his arms over his chest and heaved a frozen breath into the morning air. The same thought that had plagued him since he was a boy struggling to control the brute bear cub in his middle flashed through his mind again. Maybe he was broken.

Alana looked up, her dark skin practically glowing in the muted light from the sunrise behind him. Today, she'd curled her hair and left it down except for a few pieces she'd pinned back from her face. She was about seven levels out of his league, and yet here she was, catching his eye, a slow, greeting smile spreading across her lips.

Damn, he was in trouble with this one. He should leave. He should give her a shot at happiness with someone normal.

It was too late for escape when Alana pushed open the door to her shop, steaming coffee pot in her hand and a questioning quirk to her dark, delicate eyebrows. "I thought for a minute you were standing me up."

Aaron ran his hand along the back of his head and ducked his gaze. The thought had crossed his mind. "I'm maybe not the best company right now. Can we meet up when I'm more...?"

"More what?"

"In control." Nope, he wasn't showing his eyes right now. They were likely damn near gold, the color that usually terrified small children and protective mothers. And he couldn't stomach the idea of scaring Alana.

"Hey," she murmured, approaching slowly.

Aaron winced and angled his face away from her. "Don't."

He thought she would say something, pop off maybe, but she didn't. Instead, she slid her hand around his waist and rested her cheek against him. Chest heaving, Aaron closed his eyes and prayed for control as he settled his open palm onto the lower curve of her back.

He owed her some sort of explanation, but hell if he knew how to explain Bear to a human. "Someone died. A man."

"Last night?"

He jerked his chin once.

"Do you want to talk about it?"

He shook his head slowly as she ran her nails lightly up and down his spine.

"Okay, we won't talk about it then. But let me feed you before you go back to Nantahala."

He leaned back and frowned down at her. "How do you know I live there?"

Ignoring his question, she said low, "I like your eyes this color." As she searched his gaze, she didn't look or smell terrified. She looked awed.

And little by little Bear settled. Baffled by his animal's reaction, Aaron explained, "They get like this after bad shifts at the station."

"Understandable."

It was?

Alana tugged his hand and led him into the coffee shop. The patrons were staring, but she clipped out, "Get on back to eatin'," and her customers did just that.

There were three full tables on one side, so Aaron sat in a booth on the far wall to make the humans more comfortable. Even if they didn't have the instincts he did, they could tell when a predator shifter was worked up. He'd learned that over the years. It was in their subtle behaviors when he got too close to a Change in public. Even if they didn't realize they were afraid, they would shift their weight away from him, or cross to the other side of the street with confused frowns on their faces.

But then there was Alana. He could feel the heaviness of his own dominance thickening the air around him, but she'd approached him slow, like she knew what he needed, and hugged him. Settled him.

He inhaled deeply as he watched Alana pile pastries onto a plate and pour a cup of fragrant coffee, and on the exhale, he felt lighter, relieved almost. The scent of vanilla was strong and relaxing in here. Maybe that's why she smelled like that, from baking.

Under her breath, she hummed softly as she bustled over to him. Today she was wearing a pair of dark wash jeans that clung to her curves, a pink button-down blouse and matching apron with the logo for the coffee shop.

"I was thinking about not coming," he admitted

as she set down the plate of frosted strawberry pastries and the mug of hot coffee. Keeping anything from her felt wrong.

"I could tell."

She didn't sound mad, though. When she made to move off again, Aaron lost his damned mind and reached out, grabbed her hand, pulled her back slowly to him. Her reaction was perfect. An easy giggle, and then she ran her nails through his hair, smoothing it back from where it had fallen in his face. She cupped his cheek, rasped her touch down his unshaven jaw, and prettily arched her eyebrows. Her full lips turned up in the corners. Alana wielded magic. What else could explain just a touch of her hand offering him such salvation from the bad night he'd had?

Aaron angled his head and rubbed his cheek against her hand in an affection only shifters would understand the importance of. As Alana slipped away and sauntered off to help a customer who'd just come in, she swished her sexy hips with each step, as if she knew he was watching her leave.

Done. Aaron was done for. Heaving a breath, he relaxed back against the bench seat and shook his head in disbelief. If Alana even knew how much Bear had settled under her touch, or how he was slowly devoting himself to her, she would run away and never look back.

She didn't seem like a woman to play games, but Alana sure knew how to make him want to chase her.

# SEVEN

Why was she so nervous? Alana had never had the shakes like this in all her life. Talking to people had never scared her, but just the thought of refilling Aaron's coffee sent a tremble of anticipation up her spine and made her hands shake even harder. Her heart felt like it was going to gallop right out of her chest cavity. And he was a shifter! He would hear her pounding pulse.

She waved goodbye to the last table of customers and poured herself a mug of coffee, then dumped cream and sugar into it until she could stand the taste. It was ironic that she ran a coffee shop but didn't like the flavor of coffee.

Aaron had finished his breakfast and sat with his elbows resting on the table, hands cupped around his mug, staring out the open blinds to the parking lot with a faraway look in his eyes.

"A penny for your thoughts," she said as she sat across from him.

He huffed a laugh and eased back. "They aren't worth that much, I'm afraid. What happened with Doucheface?"

Alana sipped her steaming cup. "Nothing to tell, really. He wasn't my type."

"Didn't meet the list requirements?"

"Ha! He didn't meet a single one."

It was then she noticed the exhaustion in Aaron's eyes. Oh sure, he was putting on a good show, complete with smiles and nods, but he looked thrashed. Well, he *had* been up most the night with that wreck.

"Why were you crying last night?" he asked, gaze on the half-full mug cupped in his hands.

"Because I'm a wimp. I let him get to me—"

"Why?"

She sighed out a pathetically human-sounding

growl and said, "Because he mentioned my scar. He was rude about it. I'm not a fan of rude people. There is a difference in being honest and saying what's on your mind, and saying something just to hurt a person."

Aaron nodded slowly, and seconds of silence stretched between them. "What happened to your lip?"

Ah, there it was, and she didn't want him feeling sorry for her, so she sipped her coffee and formed a perfect answer before she spoke again. "I was born with a cleft lip and a cleft palate. I had four reconstructive surgeries when I was a kid to fix it, and now I don't even notice."

Aaron stretched his legs under the table, brushing her calf with his. Then blandly, he said, "Lie."

Crap. "I don't want to talk about it. I don't want that to be the only thing you see when you look at me."

"What do you see when you look at me?" Aaron asked, his blond brows high and daring her to fib again.

"Your eyes first, then your lips, hair, tattoos,

muscles, height. In that order."

Aaron flicked his fingers at her. "Eyes, lips, tits, soft skin, hair, vanilla scent, ass, tits again, then your scar. You telling me about it won't change the order. Your eyes have me first regardless."

Alana studied him carefully, but he didn't seem to be the type to bullshit. "Lissa is my twin sister, and she was born perfect. Perfect skin tone, perfect lips, thinner, shorter. The cleft lip is genetic, from my mom, and they knew before I was even born that I had it. I looked...wrong...in the ultrasounds. So Lissa was the beautiful one, and I was the one who needed all the surgeries to look like this." She gestured to her face. "I got bullied in school, and I didn't want to be in photos when I was a kid. In high school, I figured out I had to use my personality to gain friends, where Lissa just naturally made them. I love her, and I know she sometimes hates being the 'okay' twin. She found her husband Todd and married him right out of college, and they have three beautiful girls, but I'm still here, stuck in a rut, spinning my wheels and thinking if I'd have loved myself earlier, maybe I could've let someone else love me, too. I get scared that I missed my window. It's part of the reason I'm moving. Lissa

lives in Asheville, and I've never been away from her.
I never had space to see if I could be okay on my own.
She's busy with her life, but she still wants me here.
It's like that for most twins, wanting to stay close. I'm
her safety blanket, but sometimes I don't want to be. I
just want to be Alana." Heat rushed into her cheeks.
Appalled at all she'd just exposed, she took a long
gulp of her coffee and looked everywhere but Aaron.

Aaron leaned forward and ran a hand through
his hair, loosening it to flop over to the side and into
his face. "I was a firefighter in Breckenridge with my
dad's crew. Firefighting is a family thing. Sooo...I
didn't know my dad until I was five, and he didn't
know about me. Him and my mom had this one-night
stand, and then I came along as a result. My bear was
out of control when I was a cub, clawing my mom,
and I was on the fast track to biting her and Changing
her on accident. So she brought me to my dad, and
the Breck Crew, for guidance. And she and my dad fell
head over heels for each other so we stayed. But for
some stupid reason, because I'd missed out on my
first five years with my family and my cousins, I had
this urge to prove that I was good enough to be in the
Breck Crew. That I was good enough to be Cody

Keller's son. I have two younger sisters, and they just accepted their place in the crew right away. From day one, they were Breck Crew. I worked my way through Fire Academy and through all the paramedic classes and certifications because I thought if I was good enough at the family business, it would prove I'm good enough to be my father's son. But the longer I do this, the more I see the differences in my bear and my family's animals. My dad and uncles are so in control all the time. And with me...I'm fighting to look normal on the outside every minute of the job. So, you see, I know about not feeling like you belong, Alana." He lifted his earnest, sky blue eyes to hers. "But from the outside looking in? You look like you have everything together. I understand the need to move away and start over and escape shadows, but..." He spun the mug slowly on the table and frowned.

"But what?" He'd been about to ask her to stay, right?

"I'd still like to be your friend until you leave." He winced his lips up into a pained smile and leaned back, pulled his leg away from hers.

And there it was. The shutdown Aaron was

probably famous for. Had anyone really broken through his hard exterior? He seemed like a man who kept everything close to the chest, protected. He'd given her a glimpse of his real self, a peek into the window of his soul, and then yanked the blinds closed. The shift felt like jumping into a cold swimming pool after an hour in the hot tub.

She wanted to call him out and beg him to say what he really meant, but his jaw clenched with stubbornness, and she knew she'd lost the moment. So she told him instead, "I'd like that." Because being friends with Aaron was better than nothing at all.

# EIGHT

"You're a complete slob," Aaron muttered as he picked up a pile of Alana's clothes and set them on the chair in the corner of her room.

Alana giggled and pulled another box out of her closet. "Your insults don't sting me, Keller. My kitchen is clean. I just like to try on clothes in the morning."

"And you don't put them back on the hanger as you go?"

Alana ripped the tape off the box labeled *old shit*. Maybe it was in here. Yes! With a grin, she rifled through the rolled posters until she found the one she wanted. "Swear not to make fun of me," she demanded as she waved the thin roll in the air teasingly.

"Oh God, is that the poster of me?"

"It totally is! And now you're standing in my room." She puffed air out of her cheeks and murmured low, "Aaron Keller is in my bedroom."

He chuckled low in his throat and snatched the rolled glossy paper out of her hand. He pulled the rubber band off and tucked it in his pocket, the neat-freak, and then unrolled it. He let off a bellowing, single laugh and gave her the strangest look. "Are these lipstick marks?" He turned it around and pointed to his fourteen-year-old smiling lips, and sure enough, it was stained in her favorite and only lipstick color she had experimented with in middle school.

"Abort mission!" she yelped and ripped the poster out of his hands. Yep, she'd totally forgotten she used to make out with his poster.

Mortified, she started wadding up the poster, but he pulled it from her destructive grasp and shook his head. "Hell no, you don't. We're hanging this up." He sauntered out the door, shoulders shaking with his laughter as he smoothed the wrinkles from the edges.

"Where's your tape."

"I'm not hanging that."

"Why not?"

"Because I'm really embarrassed now! Can we please just throw it away and pretend this never happened?" She lunged for the damning poster, but Aaron blurred it out of the way and held it too high for her to reach. Son of a mother-fluffin' biscuit-eater.

She bounced around like an irate bunny, but she only successfully jiggled her boobs around and got a mere three inches off the carpet. Finally giving up, she crossed her arms and tried to look severe. "We're *not* okay, Aaron."

He smirked, spun on his heel, and started digging through her kitchen drawers. And damn it all, he found the tape in the second one. He probably smelled it with his super-sensitive bear schnoz, and now she couldn't meet his eyes because he really was plastering the poster of himself onto the living room wall. Alana wanted to crawl under a rock and hide forever and ever.

Aaron stood back and admired his handy work. He was still laughing, the brute. "It wouldn't have worked out with us, you know? I was a little shit when I was fourteen. Plus, I would've been prejudiced against your slobby ways."

"Well, I'm prejudiced against all of your tattoos, Aaron Keller. I mean, did you have to cover up all your damned skin with...what are those? Skulls?" She strode off murmuring under her breath, "If my daddy knew I was hanging out with a tatted-up bad boy, he would have steam blowing out of his ears."

"Oh, I'm a bad boy now?"

"Yes! And I'm a good girl."

"No, you aren't."

She went to furiously scrubbing an already clean dish in the sink just to have something to do other than shoot mind lasers at Aaron. "Yes, I am. I read books, pay all my bills on time, and pick up my nieces from school on Fridays so Lissa can get a date night with Todd. I eat well, have a consistent and early bed time, say please and thank you—"

"Who says I don't do that stuff?"

"You ride a bike that everyone hears when you coast down the street." She jammed her finger at the faint holes in his ears. "Piercings for everyone to see, tattoos everywhere, a haircut that makes you look like a hellion, and eyes that glow like the freaking sun and let everyone know you have a monster grizzly bear just waiting to rip out of you. You're a bad boy if I've ever seen one. Dangerous. Probably slept with a hundred groupies."

"You're so fuckin' cute when you're mad."

Alana dropped the ceramic plate in the sink and spun around. "*And* you cuss."

Aaron snorted. "You like when I cuss, and you like everything else. I can smell your arousal. Every time I touch you, you smell like pheromones. And if you're such a good girl, if you're so *perfect*, why does your room look like a tornado hit it?"

"Because I was trying on clothes for you!" With a gasp, she clapped her hands over her mouth and wished with everything she had she could gulp those words back down.

It was too late, though. They were out there, dangling between her and Aaron, and now his lips thinned into a straight line. He cast his attention to the open door of her bedroom, and when he looked back at her, his eyes were a muddy gold. "Explain."

She swallowed hard and let her hands fall away from her face. This was where he would run, and there was no escaping his question.

"Alana," Aaron said, angling his head in warning. "Just say it."

"You ruined everything."

Aaron locked his arms against the small kitchen table that stood between them, his triceps bulging as he trapped her in that inhuman gaze of his. He froze there, like a predator about to pounce on an unsuspecting prey, and chills blasted up her arms.

*Be brave. Don't let him see you weak.*

"I had a plan, and I was excited about letting the lease to my coffee shop and apartment go. I promised Lissa I would try a few more dates with guys in the area, just so she would feel like I tried my hardest, and then she was willing to let me move wherever I wanted, no complaints, just support. And that's a really big deal to me. Trey was my last date, and then I could've moved on guilt-free. But the whole damned time, I was comparing him to you and staring at the firehouse, hoping I would see a glimpse of you. I was more excited about you stopping by for coffee this morning than I have been about anything in a really long time. I mean, I couldn't sleep last night. I think you almost kissed me, and I kept replaying that moment over and over. My chest wouldn't stop fluttering, and I couldn't get comfortable. So I woke up early, before my alarm, and wanted to pick out something cute to wear today. For you." Alana wrapped her arms around her middle to ward off some of the vulnerability she felt under his disconcerting gaze. "I know it's stupid because we just met, but you have to remember..." Alana gestured to the poster on the wall. "I kind of watched you grow up. And then I got to meet you, and you're better than I imagined. And I don't hate your tattoos and piercings. I actually really, really like them. Not on anyone else, but on you, they're so...perfect."

"Alana," he drawled out, warning in his voice.

"I know. It's okay. I get it. Let's just forget this conversation and hang out until I go. Best buds and all. I swear I won't fangirl out on you anymore."

"Don't do that."

"Do what?"

"Act like this doesn't change things. It's not like I don't find you attractive—"

"Do you?"

"Fuck yes, Alana." He gestured to his crotch, where indeed he had a giant erection. "It's bonerville central every time I'm around you, but I'm not meant to pair up. Especially not now."

"Why?"

"Because of my job. Because I don't have control of my animal like I should. Because I have the King of the Asheville Coven trying to kill me. Because I'm trying to find my place in a new crew. Because I won't be any good at being a mate. Because my life is fucking complicated, and I don't want you to get hurt by it!"

"Sounds like a lot of excuses that will keep you good and lonely for the rest of your life. I understand, though. Really. You aren't ready, and for me, I'm in a different place." She offered him a sad smile. "Our timing is off." *The story of my life.*

Aaron let off a low growl that filled the room and lifted the fine hairs on her arms. Right before he stole his gaze from her, his eyes turned frosty. He strode into her bedroom, and when she padded in behind him to see what he was doing, Aaron was putting her shirts onto the hangers that were scattered all over her bed.

"What are you doing?"

"Cleaning up because this is my fault."

Baffled, she asked, "The clothes?"

"Yeah, the clothes, the feelings, the almost-kiss, all of it. I fucked up."

Alana sucked in air at the pain of those last three words. "That's mean, Aaron."

"I can't do this! You smell sad, and my bear...I want to... Dammit, Alana, I told you we had to be friends. Just friends."

"Caw!" Outside the window, a big black raven sat in the small tree in her landscaping.

Alana startled hard, but Aaron snarled and yanked the curtain over the window pane. "Fuck off, Wes!"

"Who's Wes?"

"No one."

"Is that a shifter out there?" she asked, jamming her finger at the swishing curtain. He looked like the one in the tree last night. "Why is he looking through my window?"

No answer.

"Is he in your crew?"

Aaron went back to hanging shirts like she didn't exist, so she shoved him hard in the arm. "I'm not just some groupie you can ignore, Aaron. That shit doesn't fly with me. Lock up when you leave." She left her bedroom and grabbed her purse off the table by the door. Asshole could have all the silence he wanted in here. She was out on this.

The doorknob was cold in her hand as she yanked on it, but in an instant, the door slammed closed and Aaron's giant hand was splayed against the wood. "You think this is easy for me, and it's not." Alana tried to face him but Aaron held her in place and murmured, "No, just let me say this."

"Okay," she whispered, rocked by the rawness in his voice.

"I feel good around you. My animal settles when you touch me, and I haven't been able to think about anything else since I met you. And that scares the shit out of me, Alana. There is a hundred percent chance of my life hurting you. *Hurting* you, do you understand?"

No. "Yes."

Aaron wrapped his arm around her middle and rested his forehead against her neck. He inhaled deeply and let off a long breath. "I don't like you mad. Don't like you upset, but I can't help this awful feeling in my gut that I'm going to be the one to hurt you."

"Then don't. Just...don't, Aaron. I'll go easy on

you. I'll keep my expectations low, and we can just see how this goes."

He huffed a humorless laugh. "Woman, you don't understand. That's not how it works for shifters. There's no *seeing how this goes*. There's choosing a mate, or not choosing. You. Feel. Dangerous."

She rolled her eyes closed because, damn, it felt so good to hear him say something real. She didn't know about shifter instincts, or the ins and outs of his culture or nature, but she understood what he'd just said. His animal was either in or out on a mate, and she felt big to him.

She understood that feeling. Even with her dull human instincts, Aaron Keller had taken up most of the space in her heart in a matter of days.

Slowly, Alana turned in his arms. She dared a look up at him, but his eyes were averted. There was a soft rumbling sound in his chest, so she pressed her palm there. "Look at me."

Aaron grimaced, but let her see him. Green-gold eyes in a man's face would've been terrifying before she met Aaron. Now, they were just beautiful. She cupped his cheek, her palm resting on the short blond scruff there. "You don't have to hide from me."

He looked at the scar on her lip, but just as she grew self-conscious, she noticed a difference in his growl. It was softer. Content sounding, somehow. Maybe he wasn't looking at her scar like everyone else did. Maybe he only saw her lips.

Aaron dragged her waist against his and lowered his mouth to hers. His kiss was gentle, moving against hers easily. He seemed calm and steady, but inside of her, a fire had started in her middle and was expanding cell-by-cell outward. She slid her arms around his neck and parted her lips slightly for him. When Aaron brushed his tongue against hers, he tasted divine.

Suddenly, everything felt right and warm. Aaron pulled her purse off her shoulder and eased them backward toward the couch. The second the backs of his knees hit the edge, he lowered them down, holding her legs apart so she straddled his lap. Angling his head the other way, he pushed his tongue farther into her mouth, drawing a small gasp of happiness from her.

In an instant, he disconnected with a soft smack. "Are you okay?" he murmured in that deep velvet voice of his.

She smiled and nipped him. Easing back, she admitted in a shaky voice, "I'm better than okay. That was amazing."

Aaron donned a proud rooster grin. Cocky man. She hated that on anyone else, but on Aaron, there was something so sexy about it. He should be confident. He was the most stunning man she'd ever seen in her life. Feeling daring, she slipped her fingertips under the hem of his navy fire shirt and brushed his skin right over his hip.

Aaron closed his eyes for a moment and blew out a soft moan. God, she loved his reaction to her touch. Leaning forward, Aaron tugged his shirt off in one smooth motion, then pulled her hands toward him until her palms rested on his chest.

"Your skin is so warm," she mused.

"I run hot."

"I'm running hot right now, too," she said with a wicked smirk.

His smile lines deepened with that naughty grin of his. "I knew you were a bad girl."

"You stop it." She settled farther up his lap, directly over his erection, and ran her hands down his hard pecs to the rippling mounds of his abs. His muscles twitched under her hand. There was a slight trail of blond hair that led in a delicious tease from his belly button into his pants and, about now, her panties were definitely soaking. She'd never been so attracted to a man before, and Aaron was a *man*. A big, brawny, snarly, half-feral bear shifter who settled when she touched him.

Aaron brushed one of her curls off her shoulder and cupped her neck, then eased her closer. This kiss wasn't the gentle one that his first had been. This was lips colliding urgently. It was leaning back against the couch and pulling her with him until her soft breasts were flush against his hard chest. Her body took over, or perhaps it was her instinct to be closer to him. Alana rocked her hips slowly onto his, and he groaned a sexy sound deep in his throat. She could feel the thick roll of his shaft underneath her, but it wasn't nearly close enough. She'd never wanted a man like this. Had never felt such an acute desperation to be locked up in intimacy. It was as if she couldn't draw an easy breath until she touched his skin.

His hands were everywhere—her back, her upper thighs, her waist—exploring, squeezing, rubbing. Aaron was setting her body on fire, touch by touch, as though he knew just how to bring her closer to the edge.

She was rocking against him rhythmically now, the friction of their hips feeling so good. Almost too late, she froze.

Aaron's response was instant. "What's wrong?"

"I'm close…"

He grazed his teeth on her bottom lip and whispered, "Come on me." And then he pulled her hard against his body and rolled his hips against her smoothly and, dear goodness, this was happening. He was going to give her an orgasm with her pants on!

His rocking motion came harder and faster, and she buried her face against his neck, biting down on his skin as a snarl rippled out of him. So sexy, so perfect. Nothing had ever felt like this. Aaron gripped the back of her head, and she released his skin and whispered his name as her climax exploded through her body. Deep, throbbing ecstasy pounded in her middle as she bucked against him and clawed at his shoulders. And before her aftershocks were through, Aaron had settled her on her back and lowered himself between the cradle of her hips. As he kissed her, he stroked against her until she was sated. The snap of his button and the rip of his zipper was loud in the quiet of the room. Without a word, Aaron eased upward, his arm locked beside her head, and he unsheathed his long, thick erection.

"I'm close, too," he whispered as he pulled the first stroke, and damn, Alana couldn't pull her gaze away from the swollen head of his cock. She'd never watched a man do this to himself before, but her body was revving up again.

His abs flexed with every stroke, his arms were hard, his tattoos stark, and Alana wanted nothing more than to feel his warm seed spill onto her skin.

Desperately, she unbuttoned her blouse and pulled it open.

"Fuck, you're so beautiful," Aaron rasped out, his eyes blazing so bright. "Ah," he grunted, his eyes on her breasts. He shot creamy warmth onto her stomach, reared back, and pushed into his hand again. Over and over, he pumped until he was empty. His stomach muscles twitched as he locked his arms on either side of her face and lowered his forehead to hers. He sighed and sipped at her lips, and when she rolled her hips toward him, he smiled against her mouth. Without her having to ask, he unsnapped her jeans and slid his palm into her panties.

"You're so wet," he murmured. Was that pride in his voice? Cocky.

"Aaron, please," she begged, rocking her hips against his palm when he pushed his fingers down her wet folds. He brushed her sensitive nub, and now she was panting for more.

Aaron pushed two fingers into her slowly, and Alana was gone. She let off a needy sound and arched her back against the couch, desperate to be closer to him. Desperate for release under his clever touch. He filled her again and again, faster and smoother until she cupped her hand over his and clutched onto his arm with her other. "Aaron, Aaron," she chanted mindlessly as he drove her closer to climax. So much pressure. So much pleasure with every stroke, and how could anything feel this good?

She dug her nails into his arm, and his growl was unexpected. He lowered his mouth to her shoulder and clamped his teeth on her, almost deep enough to break the skin. Pleasure and pain, pleasure and pain, and oh! Her body shattered around his fingers, gripping him with each pulse of her release.

Aaron's teeth bit down harder, but it was too much. "Ouch."

Her man's response to that tiny, pained sound was instant. With a muttered, "Shit," he pulled away from her so fast he was on the other side of the room before she even registered that he'd moved.

He paced the back wall like a caged animal, his eyes blazing, his chest heaving, his cheeks flushed, and his bared teeth looking sharper than she remembered. The sound that emanated from him now drew gooseflesh up across her arms.

"It's okay. It's okay," she told him, but really, she didn't know what was happening.

"I almost bit you. I almost Turned you, Alana! It's not okay!" He paced back along the wall and grabbed his hair like he wanted to scream. "We didn't even have sex, and I wanted to bite you. I was careful, and my bear still wants to mark you. I can't do this. I have to go." He eyed his shirt on the floor beside her, but shook his head and bolted out of her house shirtless instead. "I'm sorry," he choked out right before the slamming of the door.

Alana sat on her couch completely stunned and rubbed her aching shoulder. She could feel the indentations of Aaron's teeth in her skin, and how terrifying that just millimeters deeper, and she would be Changing right now. Changing into a grizzly bear, like Aaron. She hadn't thought about claiming marks. Sure, she'd known about them, known about the shifters' instincts to mark their mates, but it hadn't even crossed her mind as she'd fallen for Aaron. He'd taken up too much headspace. Maybe he was right. Maybe she was just as dangerous to him as he was to her because whatever was happening between them was bringing out Aaron's feral side.

*I'm going to be the one to hurt you.*

She hadn't really understood his fear until now. A bite would change the course of her entire life and bind her to him completely. It would take away her plans for her future, but even scarier, it would take away her humanity.

This growing obsession between her and Aaron had the potential to burn them both up.

# NINE

*Coward!* Aaron hit the throttle on the straightaway, then slowed for the turn-in to Harper's Mountains. He sprayed gravel as he took the corner too fast, but fuck it. He evened out again and blasted up the dirt road, through the open gate, and right past 1010. He flipped off the raven flying above him, then slammed on the brakes in front of his cabin.

Weston Novak stretched his wings wide, shifted gracefully into his human form, jogged a few steps on impact, and skidded to a stop beside Aaron. His eyes blazed with fury. "I fucking told you!"

"Back off!" Aaron shoved past him and escaped

into his cabin, slamming the door behind him. Or at least he thought he escaped, but the door creaked open immediately and Aaron reminded himself to replace the broken lock the second he had a chance.

"Two dreams, and it's not like I kept them to myself, Aaron!" Weston's eyes were the color of rich earth, proof that he hadn't managed to tuck his raven away completely. "You think I like this, Aaron? It fucking sucks!"

Aaron had been pacing the kitchen, hoping Weston would wear himself out, but nope. The Novak Raven was awesome at stripping people down.

"I want to go back to normal and not think about shit I can't control, but I can't. I hit the genetic tarhole, and now I can't stop seeing that woman's face. This is your fuckin' fault."

"I've been trying to stay away from her—"

"Not hard enough. Two dreams, and this morning I had a vision in fucking broad daylight, Aaron. You're making this worse. Her face with your color eyes, and this time she was crying, man. Tears streaming down both cheeks, looking completely terrified. You're going to Turn her against her will and ruin her entire life. Leave her alone!"

"You don't' understand, Wes. You don't. You haven't felt the pull of the bond yet. A few days ago I would've been like, 'all right, done. Leaving girls alone is easy.' But Alana's different."

"How?"

"She's..."

"Say it, Aaron!"

"She's mine! She's mine, okay! And don't give me that look. Don't roll your eyes like you've never seen this before. It happens. Maybe you're jaded and don't want a mate, and hell, maybe you can convince your raven your whole life that you're better off alone. I wasn't successful in doing that! Bear wants more."

"But her? A human, Aaron?" Weston's eyes softened, and he rubbed his hand over his short, dark hair. "You could've picked any other shifter."

Aaron stared out the window and shook his head. "Weston, it's not like you think. It's not like you lay eyes on your mate and decide whether to walk away or not."

"You'll Turn her."

"I won't."

Weston slammed his open palm on the countertop. "Dammit, Aaron. You aren't listening. I've seen it clear as day. It won't be on purpose either. It'll be bloody and painful, and she'll be terrified of you. Terrified of the bear you put inside of her." A muscle twitched under his eye. "The best thing you could do for that woman is to let her go."

"What's going on?" Harper asked from the open doorway.

Great. "Nothing," Aaron muttered as he turned to wash his hands in the kitchen sink. Harper would draw in her mate with the commotion, and Wyatt would smell Alana on Aaron in seconds.

Sure enough, Wyatt shadowed the door next, then Ryder, and now the whole crew was in Aaron's tiny cabin, staring at him like he was supposed to explain every feeling he'd ever had. Sometimes he really missed the Breck Crew.

"Aaron's going to Turn a human," Weston said, his black eyes sparking in a challenge.

Fuckin' little fucker.

"What?" Harper asked. "No, no, no, we're trying to settle here, not stir up fear. You know Turning humans is still a touchy subject, Aaron."

Weston raised two fingers in the air. "I vote he picks someone else fast before he gets in too deep with Alana."

"Someone else like who?" Aaron asked, appalled.

"I don't know, Aaron! Pick literally anyone with an animal. There are a dozen eligible bachelorettes in Damon's Mountains."

Wyatt's eyes narrowed on Weston, and Ryder snorted.

Red eyebrows arched high, Ryder said, "Dear dumbass, a mating bond doesn't work like that. Don't you think if any of those females interested Aaron, he would've picked one during any of the ten summers he spent in Damon's Mountains?" He swung his attention to Aaron and grinned. "Is she hot?"

"Thank you," Aaron told Ryder, grateful for an unexpected ally, "and yes."

"So on a scale of one to ten, you would rate her tits at a...?"

Harper shoved Ryder in the shoulder. "Stop talking."

"So like a nine? Please say a nine."

Aaron scrubbed his hand down his face tiredly. "A ten. Alana's a ten."

"Cool, cool." Ryder's grin grew obnoxious. "Your pants are undone."

Shit. Aaron fastened his pants and avoided everyone's gaze.

Ryder cupped his hands in front of his chest. "So like a D cup."

Harper glared at the red-headed snowy owl shifter. "I'm literally going to eat you if you don't shut up."

Ryder placed a hand beside his mouth and whispered, "She's on her period."

The single click of Harper's firestarter echoed through the cabin, and Ryder yelped and bolted out the door.

One down, three nosey crewmates to go.

"Look," Wyatt said, yanking the door to Aaron's refrigerator open. "It sucks that she's human, and it complicates things, but Wes, this one isn't any of your business."

"Except I get to have all these visions about it."

"And that's unfortunate, but you are clinging too hard to the idea that you can change the future, destiny, fate, whatever. Beaston never does that." Wyatt shut the door and popped the cap off a bottle of beer. "It's not your job to change the future, Wes. I know you're struggling to adjust to the sight, but you can't control what Aaron's going to do any more than I can control what that one is going to do." Wyatt gestured to Harper and offered her a wink. "From my experience—"

"Oh, you have visions often?" Weston asked, fury tainting his words.

Wyatt took a long swallow of beer, gulped, and then continued. "From my experience *with the bond*, running from it, or trying to tear yourself away from a mate your animal has chosen, is pointless. If Aaron's in it, he's in it, and there is nothing you or I or anyone else can say to stop it."

"Harper could order him away from her," Weston said low. He stared at Harper's sneakers instead of meeting her eyes.

"But I won't, and you know it," Harper said softly. "That's not what an alpha does, Wes."

"You don't protect human life? Because that's what I'm trying to do. I don't want more attention on us. We have the vamps and wolves lying low right now, but you and I both know they're just biding their time. The last thing we need right now is the humans turning against us, too."

Harper gathered her long dark hair at the nape

of her neck and sighed. "I'm not ordering you away from her, Aaron, but I think you should bring her here and let all of us meet her. Show her what your life is really about and give her a choice to be a part of it or not. And if you Turn this woman without her consent, you will pay in a pound of flesh. Are we clear?"

Aaron angled his jaw, exposed his neck, and nodded. "Yes." He dared a look directly into his alpha's oddly colored eyes. "We're clear."

# TEN

"Did you add the extra gravy?" Alana asked, narrowing her eyes teasingly at the short-order cook who manned the kitchen of Drat's Boozehouse. "Last time you forgot my extra gravy, and I still haven't forgiven you, Carl."

"Woman, let me live that down! Damn." The stout, thin-haired man gave her a megawatt grin and said, "I added two sides of gravy just for you."

Alana peeked into the paper bag and said, "Oooh, Carl, you're an angel sent straight from heaven."

"Uh oh," the dark-headed man beside her said. "Extra gravy?"

"Don't judge me, Kane."

"No judgement here," he said from behind his sunglasses. He always wore them, even at night, and even inside. Rumor was he had some scary-ass dragon eyes, but no one had actually seen his inner beast. Kane jerked his chin at the to-go bag on the counter. "The only time I've ever seen you order Carl's chicken fried steak and extra gravy was because something had knocked you on your ass."

"Okay, first off, aren't bartenders supposed to be like therapists? Hush hush with their client's problems and not rubbing them in their faces?"

Kane ran his hand through his dark hair, flipped it to the other side, and then looked up in the direction of the television behind the bar. Women's soccer was on. "Well, I'm not a bartender anymore, so now I don't have to mind those rules."

Alana frowned and sank onto the barstool next to him. "Did you get fired?"

Kane chuckled and shook his head. "I was only picking up extra shifts for money."

"For what? I've seen your shit-shack. It can't be that expensive," she said with a wink.

"Who's judgmental now?" At least Kane's smile

was more genuine. "I was earning money to help out a friend." He cleared his throat and amended, "I mean an ally. It's complicated. Spill your gravy story, and I'll buy you a drink. I need some entertainment other than my team getting their asses kicked by Germany." He dragged his attention from the television to her. "Deal?"

Alana looked longingly at the exit. She'd planned a long night of eating her weight in carbs, snarfing rocky road ice cream out of the carton, giving herself a pedicure, and then watching a rom-com in her baggiest, most unflattering pajamas. But maybe this was good, unloading to a stranger. Sure, she'd known Kane for a couple years. Everyone knew everyone in a small town, but the supposed dragon shifter with the deep limp on one side was a bit of a mystery to everyone. He was notorious for being a good listener, but also for never sharing a single thing about himself. So, in that regard, he really was a stranger.

"Fine. I want a Whiskey Sour, and I want extra maraschino cherries."

Kane snorted but gave her order to the new bartender whose nametag read *Bubba*.

Drat's was hopping tonight, but it was always

busy on Thursday nights. To keep her story quiet, she scooted closer to Kane and lowered her voice. "I fell into *like* with a guy, but he and I come from two totally different worlds."

Kane's face remained blank of the shock she'd expected from him, and he slurped loudly on what looked like an Old Fashioned. She'd thought her Romeo and Juliet-esque love scandal would've earned her at least an impressed eyebrow raise, but nope.

So she continued. "He's like you—"

"Wait, what do you mean like me?"

"A...you know...shifter."

"That's a dangerous game you're playing," he said in an odd tone.

"Yeah, I get that now, but it hasn't stopped my feelings for him. Which don't even matter because he freaked out and left my house after we...kissed...and it's been two days, and he hasn't called or stopped by my café, nothing. Just, no contact. He cold-turkey cut me off."

"Oookay, what's his name?" Kane asked, his voice gravelly.

"Aaron."

Kane had been in the middle of stirring his ice

with two tiny straws, but froze at the name. "Aaron Keller?"

Alana scrunched up her nose. "Yeah."

Kane huffed a surprised sound and then gave a come-hither gesture with a flick of his fingertips to a man readying to break the balls on one of the pool tables.

"I'm not your dog, Blackwing. Ask me politely," said the musclebound man with the bright blue eyes as he leaned forward to line up his shot.

Kane muttered, "Fuckin' asshole," then a little louder, "can you please come here and clear something up?"

The clack of the pool balls breaking was so loud and powerful, Alana jumped. And then the giant muttered something much too low for Alana to hear, kissed a dark-headed woman waiting her turn, shoved a red-headed titan in the shoulder playfully, and sauntered over toward them.

"Holy balls, he's coming this way." In a whisper-scream, Alana told Kane, "I'm not discussing my life with someone I've never met before!"

"Wyatt James of the Bloodrunner Crew, this is Alana Warren of the human variety."

Wyatt's eyebrows went up, and he muttered, "Oh, shit!" And then he shook her hand hard enough to rattle her teeth together. "Nice to meet you. Aaron's told us about you." He twisted his torso and whistled sharply at the others while Alana rubbed her sore hand.

"So Aaron is in your crew?" she asked.

Wyatt nodded. "Her crew, actually." He jerked his chin at the pretty brunette who was approaching with an easy smile.

"Your crew?" she asked, stunned. She'd never heard of a female alpha, but one look at her eyes, and Alana had the feeling this woman was much more than she seemed. She had one soft brown human eye, and a blue dragon eye.

"Harper," she introduced herself. Her hand was hot as lava when Alana touched her, so she made it a quick shake and then cooled her palm on the ice-filled Whiskey Sour Bubba had just set in front of her.

"I'm Alana," she murmured, shocked at meeting Aaron's crew without him. This should probably be awkward because of Aaron's finger-bang-and-run, but it wasn't.

"I'm Ryder," the redheaded giant introduced

himself. But instead of shaking her hand, he stood beside her and held out his phone in front of them. "Smile," he directed. "We're gonna make Aaron so jealous."

She gave a smile she was pretty sure looked like a grimace, the phone clicked, and Ryder went to poking buttons on his phone.

"Uh, I'm pretty sure Aaron won't be jealous, though. We parted weirdly. He stopped talking to me."

"He didn't stop on purpose," a man with bright green eyes and a camouflage baseball cap said from behind the others. "He's out of town right now."

"That's Weston," Wyatt said.

"Hi, Weston," Alana said. "Wait. Weston. Wes? Are you a raven shifter?"

"How did you know?" Harper asked, her eyes narrowing with suspicion.

Weston shook his head in warning, and his eyes darkened, so Alana covered for him. Instead of tattling to his alpha about Weston the Peeping Raven, she shrugged and answered, "Just a lucky guess."

"Aaron's definitely jealous." Ryder chortled with glee and held up his phone. There was a string of middle finger cartoons from someone called *Butt-Monkey*. Aaron, she would venture a guess.

She scrolled up and read Ryder's first message. "Hey Aaron, I just found my future ex-girlfriend. Definitely a ten. Claimed."

Alana laughed and shook her head as the others ordered drinks from Bubba.

When she turned around, Kane had moved down to the end of the bar and was watching the game again.

Wyatt followed her gaze. "He prefers solitude."

There was something tragic about that, being in a bar full of people just like him but keeping himself separate.

"You said Aaron went out of town?" she asked Weston as he settled at the bar beside her.

"Asheville needed some volunteers at their fire department to cover for a bunch of the firefighters that got food poisoning. His Fire Chief sent him and Bryant up yesterday."

Oh. "Well, he could've let me know what was going on."

Weston pulled his phone from his back pocket and hit a speed dial number. "You don't strike me as a woman who waits around for a man to call."

Well, she wasn't, but how Weston had come to that conclusion after just a few words between them, she had no clue. He slid his ringing phone over toward her.

"Hey, Wes," a deep, familiar timbre answered.

In a rush, Alana scooped up the phone and said, "Hey."

"Alana? Woman, do you ever pick up the phone at the coffee shop?"

"Well, no. It's in the office, and I'm usually busy up front or in the kitchen."

"I thought you were pissed at me and ignoring my calls on purpose. I didn't have your cell number. Look, we need to talk. I've been going nuts up in Asheville thinking you hated me. I'm on my way back to Bryson City right now. Are you gonna be up late tonight?"

She sighed, expelling a hundred pounds of stress with the breath. He wasn't mad at her, or ignoring her. He wasn't shutting her out. Aaron had just been working. "Don't you tease me and not show up. I have ice cream at the apartment and a pretty new nail polish. We can best-friend it."

"Fuck the friends talk. You and I both know that's off the table now." Was that a spark of humor in his voice?

"I don't know what you're talking about," she said coyly.

"Can I come over?" he asked.

Alana gave Weston a sideways glance, but he was busy talking to Ryder now. Softly, she murmured into the phone, "Come over me? I do believe you've already covered that base. Splurt splurt."

Aaron blasted a single laugh, then lowered his voice. "Yeah, that escalated fast. I can't stop thinking about it." Static sounded through the speaker, like he was holding the phone to his shoulder. There was also faint talking in the background.

"Where are you?" she asked.

"Filling up on gas. The attendant is looking at me right now like I'm about to rob the place."

"Well, you look like a criminal."

"Accept the tattoos, woman. They aren't going anywhere. Say yes. Come on, Alana. Say yes."

She could imagine him there, boot on the curb as the gas nozzle hung from the tank of his bike, the smile she heard in his voice stretching his lips as he waited for her answer.

She let him dangle for a moment before she gave in. "Fine. I'm not dressing up for you this time, though. You'll have to win that effort back."

"Great. Wear nothing. I'll be there in an hour. Don't let Ryder hug you." Aaron swallowed audibly over the line, then said, "I like you." And then the line went dead, as if he'd hung up before he could take it back.

A mushy squeal bubbled up her throat as she shrugged her shoulders up to her ears. He liked her!

Weston's eyes were on her lips when she handed him his phone back and murmured her thanks.

There was a furrow of worry between his dark brows, but Weston was polite enough when he said, "You're welcome."

Over the next half an hour, she nursed her drink and settled in to the easy banter of the Bloodrunner Crew. She, Alana Warren, frail human, sat in the middle of a rough-and-tumble crew of shifters and held her own. And no one blatantly stared at the scar on her lip while she talked, and no one treated her any differently because she didn't have an animal inside of her.

When she stood to leave, she pulled the money out of her pocket to pay for her to-go order. Aaron's paperclip fell out onto the floor. "Oh no!" She knelt down to retrieve it, but Harper squatted down in a blur and picked up the old rusty trinket first.

Harper got the strangest expression on her face as she stared at it. "Is this Aaron's?" she asked as soft as a whisper.

"He gave it to me."

Harper's unnerving eyes jerked up to hers, and a slow smile spread across her lips. "Do you know what this is?"

She thought it was just a little piece of trash he'd given her from his pocket on a whim, but from the way Harper was acting, perhaps it was something bigger. Alana shook her head.

"When Aaron was a kid, he would collect little treasures. And the first time he met his dad, he gave him a paperclip. And big old dominant Breck Crew alpha, Cody Keller, still carries that old paperclip wherever he goes." Harper pressed the bent metal into Alana's palm and closed her fist around it. "Aaron started carrying this one when he figured out how much it meant to his dad, and it's been his good luck charm ever since. We all used to tease him about it as a kid, but he didn't care. If he gave it to you, you're something special, Alana." Harper helped her up and held out her palm.

"You want the paperclip?" Alana asked, confused. She definitely wasn't going to part with it now, or ever, after Harper had enlightened her what it really meant to Aaron.

"Nope. Your phone."

Alana pulled it out of her purse and handed it to Harper so fast she almost dropped it.

Harper fiddled on there for a couple minutes and then handed it back. "Now you have all of our numbers, including Aaron's. He's my cousin, and I was kind of afraid he would never like someone like this. I was scared he would never connect, you know?" Harper hugged Alana's shoulders tight, warming her skin with just the brief embrace. "You call me if you ever need anything."

"Okay, I will," Alana said, eyes bugging out of her head as the alpha of the Bloodrunner Crew released her. "Um, Harper? If you ever feel like coming to Bryson city early, coffee is on me at the café. It's just down the street. It has my name on the sign out front."

"I'll visit you this week," Harper promised. "I need someone to talk about normal stuff with. I don't know any ladies around here yet, and I need a break from all the fart jokes."

Ryder looked at his alpha with a truly offended expression. "What's wrong with fart jokes?"

Harper sighed tiredly and squeezed Alana's hand, offered her a *see-what-I-mean* look, then made her way toward the door with the glowing red exit sign above it.

As Alana waved off the Bloodrunner Crew and watched them file through the door and out into the night beyond, another layer of confusion settled into her chest.

Tonight had just made her decision to move or stay even harder.

# ELEVEN

~~Popcorn~~
~~Hair in a messy bun~~
~~Sexy leopard-print push-up bra~~
~~Cherry flavored lip gloss~~
~~Cutest pajama set~~
~~Mood music~~
*Romantic comedy*

Alana checked the TV, the glowing screen paused on the opening credits of a classic mushy movie. With a satisfied sigh, she marked out the last of her to-do list with a purple gel pen. Then she tossed the scribbled paper into the trash just as a knock sounded on the door. She took a moment to ball her hands up and run in place, silently squealing with excitement. Too much energy. She had to get herself under control or she would start shaking in front of Aaron. *Be cool.*

Alana tiptoed over to the mirror right beside the door, checked herself once, then blew out three quick breaths before she pulled open the door.

Her disappointment was instantaneously consuming. It wasn't Aaron at the door, but a tall, lanky man with brown mussed hair and the same navy blue Bryson City Fire Department shirt Aaron wore on his shifts.

Her heart dropped to the ground as realization suddenly flooded over her. "Is Aaron okay?"

"Yeah, yeah, of course. Sorry. I'm not here with bad news, and I'm really sorry it's so late." He put his hands on the doorframe and looked around inside her house. "I'm a friend of Aaron's and was wondering if I could come in and talk to you for a minute? It's important."

"It's midnight."

"Yeah." The man linked his hands behind his

neck and gave her a charming hot-guy grin. That shit would've worked on her last week, but Aaron's was better. "Again, I'm so sorry about the time. Can I come in?"

"I'm not comfortable with that. I'm glad to meet another friend of Aaron's, but whatever you need to talk about, you can do from there. Or tomorrow. Tomorrow would be good."

The man's eyes flashed with a surprising coolness for just a moment before it was gone. He looked down the street and let off a laugh that echoed around her porch and bounced around in her head. Chills rippled up her spine, and with a gasp, she shoved the door to close it.

"*Stop.*" The word was clear as a bell, but the man's mouth hadn't moved from the cruel, twisted smile.

Alana stood frozen, holding the edge of her door, trying and failing to move a single muscle to close it.

"*You don't want to do that. Don't want to do that. Don't want to.*" The deep, dark words tumbled over each other in her mind. "*Invite me in. Invite me. Invite me in, Alana Warren.*"

*Fuck you.* She wanted to say it so badly. The

words sat there on the end of her tongue, ready like ammunition in the chamber of a gun. But when she forced air past her vocal cords, all that came out was, "Won't you come in?"

She whimpered as her traitorous hand opened the door wider.

The man wore a pleased expression as he murmured, "Good girl," and stepped one echoing, ominous boot onto her wooden floors, then shut and locked the door behind him.

Linking his hands behind his back, he made his way slowly around her living room, looking at this and that while Alana stood plastered against the wall, no more mobile than the old sconce beside her cheek. She tried with everything she had to move a single muscle. Just one, so she could be in control of her body again, but she couldn't. "Wh-who are you?"

"I'm Aric." He turned to her and lifted his chin proudly. "I'll be your maker."

"No." Her eyes burned with the realization of what he was. Of what she'd stumbled into. *Vampire.* No, no, no, this wasn't happening. Alana sucked in air and screamed, "Aaron!"

Aric disintegrated into hundreds of fluttering,

flapping bats immersed in a thick, purple smoke, the tendrils reaching for her.

"Help me!" she screamed.

Aric appeared in front of her, inches away, and cupped his hand roughly over her mouth, stifling her shriek. "Shhhh." Aric canted his head and dipped his gaze to her neck. "The last leader of my coven liked pain. She liked people to scream while she drank them up, but I'm not like her. Don't be scared. Don't cry. This won't hurt much. I'll be gentle and fast, and when you wake up, you will have paid the Bloodrunner Dragon's debt."

Alana opened her mouth to tell him she didn't understand. To beg him not to do this, not to hurt her, but as his lips curled back, her words died in her throat. His teeth were razor sharp, growing longer by the second.

She was going to die here, alone with this monster. She wouldn't be able to say goodbye to her dad, Lissa, or her nieces. There would be no more breathless moments with Aaron. There would only be pain, and then nothing at all.

"You're going to stay still for me, won't you Alana? So I don't hurt you any more than I have to. No screaming. Say it."

He pulled his hand off her mouth, and she choked on the words as she repeated, "No screaming."

*Move body! Do something! Don't just stand here and die!*

An almost-human emotion flitted across Aric's eyes—regret perhaps—before he inhaled deeply and leaned into her. She could feel the warmth of his breath and the sharp points of his fangs. A single tear slipped down her cheek as she fought off the vision of Aaron's lips right before he'd kissed her. Her mind was trying to run to something good, but he didn't belong here in this dark moment. She couldn't taint her memory of Aaron like that.

Pain, pain, pain and then…nothing.

Aric blasted backward and broke clean through the sheetrock of the opposite wall. Bats poured from the hole, squeaking a sickening sound as the arms of smoke flowed this way and that. Aaron stood in front of her now, his shoulders looking even more massive as he clenched his hands and heaved breath.

Alana slid to the floor on her numb legs as a wave of bats circled Aaron. "No," she whispered, desperate to claw her way toward him. She had to do something, but Aaron didn't need her help. He reached into the smog with unbridled focus and precision, and then slammed something onto the floor so hard the boards shook beneath her. Aric's form solidified, his throat in Aaron's hand. Aaron's muscles bulged as he squeezed.

"Please. Don't!" Aric begged, and it was then that she saw it. Her coffee table was toppled over, and in Aaron's grip was the fourth splintered leg, pressed against Aric's chest right over his heart.

"Tell me why I shouldn't give you your final death," Aaron growled in an inhuman voice.

"I was going to be gentle. I have to avenge Arabella. Please, just let me explain. I'm trying to avoid war!"

Aaron slammed him on the ground so hard Alana could hear the sickening crack of Aric's head. He pushed the table leg into the vampire's chest by millimeters, and behind Aric's gritted teeth came a pained keening sound, like nails on a chalkboard.

"If you kill me, that will be a queen and a king, and that can't be forgiven, Bloodrunner! It won't just be the Asheville Coven wanting revenge. You'll have the entirety of my kind fighting over your deaths. Nothing will save you then."

Aaron straddled the monster. Every muscle bulging and tense, Aaron glanced over at Alana with wild eyes. "Look away."

"Aaron, listen to him."

"Alana," Aaron warned. "Look away now."

"I care about human life! I wasn't going to kill her, only Turn her."

"She isn't yours to Turn, Aric! I fucking tried with you, man. I tried working alongside of you after all that you've done. Your queen tried to break Wyatt. Your coven came for Harper. You ripped my fucking throat out, and now this? It isn't her fate to be a monster!" Aaron roared, the veins in his throat protruding. "I've watched you work to save human life. I've seen the look in your eyes when you lose one. It affects you, so how can you do this to Alana?"

"Because we don't work like you! We don't have the same rules. A Bloodrunner killed my queen, and yeah, she deserved it. Aaah!" Aric made a choking sound as Aaron pushed on the leg of the table. "She deserved it! Arabella was too old to rule, was undergoing The Sickening, and she played with Wyatt to make her feel steady. I hated it. We all did, but she was our queen. The first rule for a new king or queen is to avenge the last! I *have* to avenge her, Aaron! I can rule my people better, but not without meeting the Rule of Vengeance. A life for a life. My people want the dragon. They want Harper, but I don't want war. This is the best I could negotiate. A life for a life. I was going to Turn Alana, not kill her. It would've satisfied the blood debt. Don't do this. Don't start a war. No one will survive."

"Fuck!" Aaron yelled, pulling the make-shift stake from Aric's chest. He shoved off him and paced to Alana, then back to the vampire. "Her fucking pupils are blown out, man. Get out of her head. Fix her. Now!"

The relief was instant. It was as if she'd been suffocating with a plastic bag over her head, and it was that glorious moment when her lungs filled with beautiful life-giving oxygen. Alana's muscles relaxed, but then tensed again when she scrambled upward, cupping her throbbing neck.

Aric was on his hands and knees now, gasping and holding his chest where he'd been inches away from wood through the heart. Aaron wasn't okay. He was snarling savagely and pacing, and the air in her small apartment was almost too thick to breath.

"She's mine, Aric."

"I know. That's why—"

"Shut the fuck up and listen! She's mine. My claim, my mate. If you can't convince your coven to leave her alone, you'll have that war. Only it won't be two hundred vamps against the Bloodrunners. I'll call in every fucking crew of shifters on the goddamn planet. Every dragon, every bear, every boar, every big cat, every gorilla, every bird of prey will be fighting for your final deaths. You won't be able to find a hole deep enough to hide from my wrath, is that clear?"

"There are rules—"

"Aric, I'm saving your people from extinction right now when all I want to do is stake you and piss on your fucking ashes. Yes or no? Is. That. Clear?"

The vampire's eyes glowed with fury in the moment before he wised up and dropped his gaze from Aaron's. "We're clear. I'll handle my coven."

"Get out."

Aaron's greenish gold eyes tracked the vampire as he strode immediately out the open doorway. The door was lopsided on the frame, held up by one bent hinge, and the small window on it was shattered. Where it had been locked, the deadbolt had ripped right through the doorframe. Aaron had forced his way in, and now she realized how much power he'd been hiding from her. She knew about vampires. Everyone did, and they were supposed to be the strongest beings on earth. Someone had lied to the humans. Aaron Keller had just cowed the King of the Asheville Coven, and he hadn't even broken a sweat.

Shifters ruled the world, and no one even knew it but them.

She had stayed strong up until the moment Aaron's attention swung slowly to her. The feral snarl was gone, and in its place, worry. "Are you okay?" he whispered, approaching her slowly.

What was the point in lying if he could sense it? "No." She looked around her apartment, which had been trashed by Aric's bats. The floor was covered in shattered glass and debris, and her neck stung like Aric's teeth were still piercing her. "I didn't mean to let him in." She hated feeling weak, and for some reason, this all felt like... "It's my fault."

"No, it's really not." Aaron shook his head, and

his blazing eyes filled with ruthless honesty. "This is his fault. It's my fault. It isn't your fault. Let me see." He pried her cupped hand away from her neck and grimaced. "Do you have a first aid kit?"

"No."

"What? Why not?"

"Because I'm not a shifter, Aaron. Maybe you bleed all the time, but I've never had more than a papercut in this apartment. I'm Steady Alana, remember? Boring life. Safe life. No bleeding, no need for first aid." She wasn't being fair. This really wasn't his fault either, but she was panicking and desperate to place the blame somewhere just to cope with what had happened.

Aaron drew her in close, crushed her against his chest. "Alana, you're okay. I swear I'll keep you safe. That'll never happen again."

She closed her eyes and clutched onto his shirt as a sob wrenched its way up her throat. How would she ever be able to feel truly okay again? Aric had controlled her mind, her body. She was supposed to be some blood-debt for the Bloodrunners, whatever that meant.

Aaron sighed and pulled her behind him to the

bathroom. He dug through the linen closet and found a washrag, then pressed it against her neck. And without any explanation, he started shoving some of her clothes willy-nilly into an oversize black tote bag.

"Where are we going?"

"To Harper's Mountains." His hand shook as he reached for a blouse on her bed, and he hesitated, clenched his fist like he was trying to steady it. "You can't stay here. Not when you've already invited Aric in. Not when the damn door is off its hinges." His voice was an unrecognizable growl now. It was clear he was struggling with something she didn't understand—his bear perhaps?

She rested her hand gently on his back, and he tensed. Locking his arms against the bed, he said, "Please don't fight this, Alana. I can't be away from you right now. I just can't."

"Okay. I want to go. I want to stay with you."

The rock hard muscles of his back relaxed fractionally, and he pulled his cell from his back pocket and told her to, "Pack what you need for tonight," as he punched buttons on the glowing screen.

The second she was finished packing her

toiletries, he shouldered her tote and pulled her through the disheveled living room and out the front door. He spent some time settling the door snugly into place, then led her at a jog around her café to the small parking lot out front where his motorcycle sat gleaming under the single street light.

"Wait, we're riding on that? Without a sidecar? Or airbags, or a seatbelt?"

"You'll be fine, I promise. I won't let anything happen to you."

And she believed him. She trusted him. He'd come for her, stood between her and that vampire, and threatened war between the two biggest supernatural bodies in the world. Aaron Keller had threatened to bring hell to earth to protect her, and every fiber of her being believed he would actually follow through.

Aaron slid his leg over the seat of his bike, jammed the kickstand up with his heal and turned the engine. It was much louder up close than she'd expected, but with only a second of hesitation, she slid her palm onto his offered one and eased onto the motorcycle behind him. Aaron adjusted the bag over his shoulder, pulled her hands around his waist, and told her to, "Hold on to me."

The warmth had stopped trickling down her neck, and the pain had eased. Her adrenaline dump had left her feeling mellow and like she was floating outside of her body. As Aaron eased onto Main Street and toward the Smoky Mountains, she rested her cheek against his back and sent a silent thank you to the heavens that he cared enough to put himself between her and that monster. He'd told that vampire she was his claim, his mate, and though she'd been too scared at the time to realize what he was declaring, it hit her like a lightning strike to the heart now.

*My claim, my mate.*

Alana held on tighter to his taut waist as he hit the gas outside of town. When the wind kicked up and something massive blocked out the stars and moon, she tensed, terrified that it was the bats back to finish her off.

"It's Harper," Aaron assured her over his shoulder. "She'll be watching over us coming in."

But he was wrong. It wasn't just Harper protecting them as they blasted toward her mountains. Alana smiled tentatively at the giant raven and snowy owl that glided alongside of them on the edge of the woods.

Alana tilted her face back and looked up into the sky at the golden underbelly of the massive dragon above. Harper's wings looked dark, a forest green perhaps. She scanned the woods around them, snaking her long neck this way and that as she thrashed her wings against the air currents.

Alana should feel scared right now. Terrified even. Her neck still burned, and her muscles remembered how awful it was to be frozen in place. But Aaron had declared her his, and the Bloodrunner Crew being here said they accepted that. They accepted her.

She'd never been in more danger in her entire life.

But somehow, someway, Alana had never felt this safe either.

# TWELVE

The throaty *pa-pa-pa* of Aaron's motorcycle slowed with their speed as he drove them through a gate Wyatt was holding open. His eyes were glowing brightly in the moonlight as he watched them pass with a nod of his head. When they were clear, Wyatt closed the gate behind them and followed the motorcycle at a jog. In a clearing up ahead, a cabin appeared surrounded by towering trees. The moon was full tonight and cast everything in a neon blue glow, so perhaps that was the reason Alana got chills when she laid eyes on the old log cabin with the sagging front porch.

"Is this your house?" she asked, awed at its ethereal beauty.

"No. Mine is up that trail." Aaron nodded at a dirt track that wound around jutting black rocks. Up the hill, she could just make out a couple more cabins in the tree line. "This," he said, jamming the kickstand down in front of the first house, "is ten-ten."

The raven spread its wings and extended its legs, and in a moment, Weston landed near them in his human form.

"Oh my God, there's a dick." A giant one, eek! Alana ripped her gaze away from Weston's tatted up, rippling, naked body only to land on Ryder, who was standing nearby with his hands on his hips and a giant erection at half-mast. The white of his teeth flashed right before she squeaked and looked away. Harper strode around the house, naked as the day she was born, perky boobs bouncing. She looked completely comfortable with her nudity, but Alana was not. "Tits and dicks," she blurted out, then buried her face against Aaron's back as he chuckled. "Can everyone put clothes back on. Please."

"Naked bodies are completely natural," Ryder explained.

She looked up to argue, but he was flapping his long pecker from side to side against his legs with a big grin on his face.

"Ryder, cut it out," Aaron muttered, but his shoulders were shaking with laughter, and this was not funny!

She would simply close her eyes. That worked until Aaron got off the bike and escaped the range of her searching hand. With a growl of utter mortification, Alana eased her eyes open, angled them at the ground *only*, and stumbled off the bike. Her legs felt like noodles after the ride in, so she bounced this way and that, hands cupped above her eyebrows so she didn't have to see all the swinging dicks. She followed Aaron's boots up the creaking porch stairs and into the open doorway.

Inside, the warm glow of the lights urged Alana's shoulders to relax. Harper was pulling on a pair of jeans near the kitchen table, and thankfully the beefy nudists outside didn't seem inclined to follow them in.

"You'll stay here tonight," Harper said.

"What?" Aaron asked. "No, I need her with me."

"Then you can stay here, too."

"I don't understand, Harper. I have a cabin right up the hill."

Harper let off a long, terrifying growl that was so loud it filled every inch of the room. "Weston asked Wyatt and I to move out of here for a reason."

Aaron drew back like he'd been slapped. "Where are you living?"

Wyatt handed Harper a sweater and told him, "We moved to the cabin at the top of the hill. The one against the cliffs."

Aaron settled his confused frown on Alana and pulled her tightly against his side. Then he murmured to Harper, "But you love ten-ten."

"And I always will, but Weston thinks there is good mojo in here."

"Harper—"

"If Alana is to find sanctuary here, it'll be in ten-ten," Weston said from behind them. He was buttoning up a pair of jeans, and when he looked up, his eyes were black as pitch instead of the bright green she'd seen in them earlier. "Aaron, you didn't grow up in Damon's Mountains, and you didn't see what that old trailer did for the mates. You think the original ten-ten gained fame because of ghost stories, but there was something about it. Something beyond this world that kept people safe. I knew these mountains were special the second I saw those numbers on the door. Your mate's neck has the bite of a vampire, and from what I'm guessing, things could've gone very differently tonight. If there's any chance of putting any good vibes on Alana, ten-ten is my vote."

Aaron's voice softened as he murmured, "I thought you were against me pairing up."

Weston huffed a hollow sound. "I wasn't scared of you pairing up, Aaron. You've picked someone fragile, though, and I don't want you losing her."

Weston turned to leave, but that last comment pissed Alana off. "I'm not fragile," she said, steel in her voice.

Weston shook his head, but didn't turn around as he said, "Not for long."

"What does that mean?" Alana asked.

Aaron's eyes were a frosty blue as he watched Weston disappear into the night. "Nothing."

But it wasn't nothing. Suddenly none of the shifters in 1010 would meet her gaze anymore, and there was something big and unspoken hanging in the air between them. Something that festered and grew heavier with every moment she waited for an explanation they refused to share.

After all she'd been through tonight, she deserved the whole story, and once again, she was being shut down. Fine. She wasn't going to stand in here like a bump on a log waiting for answers that wouldn't come. "Where's the bathroom," she gritted out. Damn her voice as it shook, but she was angry.

"Through there," Harper said, gesturing to a bedroom. "There's a first aid kit under the sink."

"Thank you." Alana yanked the strap of her tote bag from Aaron's shoulder and made her way out of the living room.

"I'll help," Aaron murmured, but Alana shut the bathroom door before he reached her.

If he was going to shut her down, she wouldn't share this part with him. This was hers to privately endure so she could wrap her head around all that had happened tonight. Alana slid her back down the cabinets and squeezed her eyes closed as her face fell. She prided herself on being a tough, independent woman, but tonight she'd gone through hell. Tonight everything had changed. Tonight had taken her on the highest highs, the lowest lows, and everywhere in between, and nothing but a good cry would make her feel better.

And if Aaron's answers to her questions were riddled with "nothings," then he wasn't allowed to see her vulnerable side.

**\*\*\*\***

Aaron paced outside the bathroom, ran his hand through his hair, and then strode to the door, determined to escape. He couldn't. Couldn't move another step away from her, couldn't lose himself to Bear right now. Not when that soft sniffle sounded through the door. It ripped him apart. She wasn't the type of woman he would be able to protect by hiding the truth, and he'd been an idiot to forget that.

What the hell was he doing?

He'd been on autopilot since he'd heard her scream his name, scream for help. The sound of terror in Alana's voice would never leave his memory as long as he walked this earth. It would replay in his nightmares over and over because he'd thought he was going to be too late. Aric had gotten too damn close to her. The rules for vampires were the same as for shifters. Legally, they could Turn one person, but only with consent, and only when choosing a mate. Alana would've been legally bound to Aric if he would've Turned her. All he had to do was convince Alana and the court that his draining her and raising her from the dead had been consensual. And he could've done it! Aric possessed the power of mind control.

"Fuck," Aaron muttered, clenching his shaking hands. The constant snarl in his chest was unavoidable now.

What was he supposed to do? Alana was crying, and he was teetering on the edge of his control. All he wanted was to hold her, but she'd shut him out, and he had no fucking clue how to make his woman happy.

He was the oldest of the Bloodrunners, in his thirties, and when the mating bond hadn't happened with any of the girls he'd dated through his twenties, he'd assumed he wasn't meant to be paired up. It happened to lots of shifters, so he'd just accepted it. Accepted that he would watch his friends find mates and be a good uncle to their kids instead of getting to raise his own. And then Alana had come along, and the pull of the bond had been instant—like slamming into a brick wall at full speed. There had been no slowing down or avoiding it. It was almost as if she'd been there all along, arms open wide, just waiting for him to crash into her.

He'd told her he didn't want to hurt her, and now look. She was the only one on the front line of a war brewing between shifters and vamps, and she was human! Weston was right about her being fragile. She was tough as hell on the inside, but her skin was thin as paper. She didn't have swift healing. And if he was honest, watching her neck streaming crimson tonight had done something awful to his insides. He hadn't realized how different it was for humans until tonight. It was one thing to know it, but another to see how easily they bled over something as simple as a bite. How easily the woman he was falling in love with could be taken from him.

Alana let off a soft, heartbroken sound, and he couldn't do it anymore. He couldn't just give her space to fall apart without him. His protective instincts wouldn't allow it. Aaron shoved the door open and dropped to his knees on the floor, pulled her into his lap. She struggled for a moment and told him to, "leave me alone," but her words didn't have any vitriol behind them. As he held onto her tighter and buried his face against her neck, she wrapped her arms around him and clung on like he was her air.

"Weston has dreams. Visions," he murmured low. "Before he even met you, he saw you with eyes the same color as mine."

As he rocked her gently, Alana's breath hitched. "What does that mean?"

"Weston thinks I'll be your maker." Aaron's voice cracked on the last word, but fuck it. She should know every single complicated thing so that she could make an educated decision whether to stay with him or leave his life forever.

"Claiming you would be big, Alana, and not something I want to do without your consent. My mark would Turn you. It's a huge commitment."

"It would be like marriage for you, right? Like a ring."

He sighed against her skin and kissed the uninjured side of her neck. "It would be bigger. For a shifter, a claiming mark is so much bigger. It's the animal choosing without a shadow of a single doubt that he will be devoted to that person forever. There is no turning back, no breaking up, no divorce, no bowing out of the relationship after that. There would only be my unrelenting devotion."

Alana was quiet for a long time, and he got it. She had so much to think about. This stuff wasn't public knowledge for humans. It was the part of shifter culture that was no one else's business but theirs. Slowly, she wiped her eyes, then straddled his lap and hugged him, resting her chin on his shoulder. "Would I feel that, too? If you claimed me, and turned me into a bear shifter, would I feel bound to you?"

He swallowed hard so his voice wouldn't crack when he answered. "Yes. And it could be amazing. It's something I want with you, but there is a trade-off."

When Alana leaned back, Aaron was struck with how damn beautiful she was. Smooth skin shades darker than his, a tone between rich caramel and milk chocolate. Her eyebrows were arched perfectly, her delicate nose slightly rosy from crying. She wore her hair all piled on the back of her head, sexy-messy, and her dark eyes were vulnerable as she searched his face. "Tell me everything."

And he did. He laid it all out there, all the scary parts of his life, all the complications. He told her about Harper going through The Unrest until they formed a crew. He told her about his excitement over fighting vamps, and how it had really been awful. He told her about the fight with the Asheville Coven in the parking lot of Drat's and the death of the queen.

"Is that where you got this?" she asked in a whisper as she brushed her fingers over the scars on the side of his neck.

He dipped his chin once. "Aric gave me that."

She touched her own bite mark. "We'll match."

"No," he said firmly. "There is a woman in the Ashe Crew who makes cream for fixing scars. I'll have some shipped here, and you won't have to remember what Aric did to you every time you look in the mirror."

"Why didn't you use it on your neck?"

"Because scars are a part of every shifter's life. We fight battles the humans are never aware of. Scars are a reminder of what happened but also a warning of what's to come. Scars mean we survived. It doesn't have to be like that for you, though. It can be easier." He lowered his voice and cupped her cheeks. "Alana, I'll make it easier, I swear."

Her lip trembled, but she kissed his palm quickly. He loved that she was tender, affected, and real. He'd had trouble connecting with his emotions over the years, trouble understanding Bear, but here was Alana, so authentic, soft, and honest, and for some reason, that little lip quiver exposed strength in her vulnerability. It was a measure of trust that she allowed him to witness the dampness on her cheeks. Allowed him to brush them away with the pads of his thumbs.

The choice would be hers, to stay and endure a dangerous life or to move away and find a normal partner who would cloak her life in the safety of normalcy. It would rip him up inside if she chose the latter, but an overwhelming desire for her to be happy had overtaken him. At least he'd laid it on the line. At least he'd told her everything she needed to know about his life to choose her path. He wasn't hiding anything anymore.

All he could do now was spend every minute possible with her until she moved away from Bryson City, or decided to stay here with him.

# THIRTEEN

Aaron was scared.

Alana didn't know how she knew it, but some instinct deep inside of her kept circling back to that thought as the seconds ticked by in the dark bedroom. He'd avoided the bed, told her goodnight, and settled on the couch outside the door. And there he lay, just on the other side of the wall. So close and much too far all at once.

He was scared of Turning her. And if Aaron was unsure if he could control his grizzly during intimacy, she should be, too. At least, that's what she'd been telling herself for the past half an hour. So why did each minute that ticked by get harder and harder to resist tiptoeing into the living room and crawling onto the couch beside him?

Alana rolled over on her side and hugged a pillow to her chest. Softly, through the dark, she asked, "Would it hurt?"

After a moment, Aaron's deep voice drifted through the open doorway. "Would what hurt?"

"You know. The bite."

He huffed a sigh, and she could make out the rustle of fabric. She could imagine him sitting up now, hands scrubbing his face. "I haven't ever thought about it before. I was born like this. I imagine it would. Shifter healing makes wounds seal up fast, but I still feel pain. Maybe worse pain because the healing happens so quickly and is so intense. Yeah, I think it would hurt."

"Bad?"

"Yeah."

"I hate pain." She rubbed her fingers lightly over the bandage on her neck. She'd taken a couple of pain killers at Aaron's instruction, but it still ached. Or maybe it was the flashes of Aric's teeth coming at her that made it sting worse. "It seems like shifters have to get used to being hurt."

The floorboards creaked under Aaron's bare feet as he sauntered into the bedroom. His hair was mussed, and the blue moonlight that streamed through the window contoured his pecs, abs, and strips of muscles over his hips in delicious shadows. He hesitated at the edge of the bed, but Alana pushed back the covers and tossed the pillow she was hugging to the other side of the bed to make room.

He looked back at the doorway, as if he was debating an escape, but Alana yanked his hand down before he could scurry away. Aaron laughed and crawled under the covers with her. How was he so warm?

Snuggling against his chest, she admitted something she had never told anyone in her life. "Lissa was always the strong one out of us."

"How so?"

"She was tough. Like when she would get sick, she didn't want anyone fussing over her. She would hole up in her room, and if anyone mentioned her having a cold or stomach flu, she would deny it and force everyone to go about their business like nothing was wrong. She hated being coddled. And then there was me." Alana laid a kiss on his chest, then murmured, "If I broke a nail, I was done for. Wailing, crying, telling my dad I thought I was dyin'. At Christmas last year, he told me I used to scare him to death because I always made him think my injuries were serious. He used to call me his 'lil drama momma."

Aaron's chuckle was deep and vibrated against her cheek.

The smile dipped from her face before she admitted the rest. "I always thought Lissa should've been the one with the cleft lip and palate. Not because I would wish it on anyone, but because she would've gone through the surgeries, no complaints, and when they were through, she would've just gotten over it. Moved on. She would've owned it a lot sooner than I did. I always wished I was strong like her."

"Mmm," Aaron rumbled. "You don't know how she would've reacted to what you went through. Not for sure. Maybe your sister got quiet about her hurts because she watched what was happening to you. Maybe she hid her pain on purpose so it wouldn't add to what your family was already going through."

"I was always a daddy's girl, too, and I got to keep him, you know? When we lost my mom, Lissa got quiet. She was closer to her than she was to Dad."

"Were you and your sister close?"

"Oh, hell yeah. Sometimes I miss how we used to be. We still talk on the phone and see each other on Fridays when I watch my nieces, but life got in the way, you know? She had a husband and then kids, but I just stayed still. Just…waiting around for whatever attention she had left to give. I guess that's part of the appeal of moving far away, so I don't have to feel like I'm just sitting around, wasting my life for a connection that can't ever be the same as when we were kids."

"Did you tell her about me?"

"Yeeees," she drawled out. "I called and told her you were tall and nice and a firefighter, but I left out the tattooed, motorcycle-riding, demon-eyed shifter part. Baby steps with her."

Aaron snorted and hugged her closer, and that was when she felt it. He was rocking one massive boner behind the fabric of his briefs.

"Good God, Aaron, is that a tree trunk, or are you happy to see me?"

"Woman, flattery gets you everywhere with me." He rested his hand behind his head and grinned. "Keep talking about my big dick, and it'll keep getting bigger."

"I meant bonsai tree trunk."

Aaron tickled her ribs, and she went to giggling and kicking at the covers. "Stop, stop!" she punched out through her laughter.

Aaron rolled smoothly on top of her, straddled her hips, and pinned her thrashing arms above her head. His eyes were too bright now, too animalistic, and his chest heaved with a sudden breath as the smile faded from his face.

He dragged his hungry gaze down her body, all the way to where their hips met, then back up to her face. "I don't want to hurt you," he whispered, releasing her arms and leaning up straight.

"You won't, Aaron. I trust you."

He shook his head, back and forth, back and forth, his eyes locked on hers. She could see a million thoughts churning there.

"Sometimes mates stay human, right?"

A slight nod.

"I'm not saying I'm out on an eventual claiming

mark, but..."

"It's a lot now, I know. Humans work differently. Feel differently. It happens slower for you."

Gathering her courage, Alana sat up just enough to pull off her tank top. Her bare breasts prickled as the cold air drifted over her skin. Slowly, she settled back onto the mattress again.

Aaron's breath came shallow as he stared. And after the span of a few heartbeats, he leaned forward, locked his arms on either side of her head, and searched her eyes. There was still an air of hesitation, so she reached up and cupped his face, demanded his attention.

"Don't bite me," she whispered. His eyes blazed brighter, so she smiled and pulled him closer. "Bear, don't claim me until I'm ready. No hurting me."

A soft rumbling growl emanated from Aaron's chest, and then he was on her, his lips crashing against hers like waves on a cliff. Fire ignited along her nerve endings, starting from where their hips met and exploding out to her fingertips. Aaron winced and drew back from her touch as if he'd felt it, too, and after an initial look of shock that likely mirrored her own, the corners of his lips curved up in a wicked smile. He intertwined his fingers with hers and slid her hands above her head as he eased down and kissed her lips again. He rocked seductively over her as he sucked her bottom lip. She was no better than putty in his capable hands. There was no room for nerves or insecurity here, not with him. He was laying claim to every thought, every breath, every reaction of her body. He eased his lips off her with a hard suck, and she gasped as her body bowed against the mattress. She *needed* to be closer to him. No man had ever affected her like this, so completely. Every cell in her body belonged to the man who had stolen her heart.

Aaron dipped his lips to her neck and drew his hand from hers, dragged his touch slowly up her arm to the bandage on her neck. He pulled it off. She didn't even feel the pull of the tape on her neck, but the second Aric's bite was exposed to air, a tingling sensation skittered across her sensitive skin. She hated what he'd done.

"I won't bite you, Alana," Aaron said in a deep, gravelly voice. "Not until you beg me to." He worked sucking kisses along her throat until he reached the torn skin. "But I'm going to show you that not all pain is bad."

Holy. Shit. Could his words make her come? Was that a thing? He was building pressure in her middle that had her panting in desperation. His warm breath on her neck teased her with how close he was to making his claim.

The cuts burned as he kissed her skin, his tongue soft as he brushed it against her. Alana was shaking now, trying not to plead with him, trying to keep her pride, but he was demolishing her defenses one touch at a time. He released her other hand, cupped the side of her neck, and when he pressed his thumb against her tripping pulse, the growl in his chest rattled harder. Sexy, beastly man.

Wanting more, she drew her knees up on either side of him. And as he worked her neck, he lowered his hips and rolled his erection against her, hitting her clit through her thin pajama pants just right.

She moaned, and he reacted, sucked too hard. She hissed and dug her nails into his shoulder as punishment. But Aaron had been right. The pain in her neck added to the pleasure he was conjuring between her legs. He ran his kisses down the length of her collar bone and settled more of his weight onto her, and now when he rocked against her this time, waves of ecstasy flooded the apex between her thighs. Squeezing her eyes closed, Alana tried to convince her body to hold on. When that didn't work, she rushed out, "Aaron!"

He smiled against her skin, then slid down her body, yanking her pants off as he went. He was lightning fast, and she froze, completely shocked that he'd suddenly disappeared from her torso and was now tossing the remainder of her clothes onto the floor. She wanted to squeak and cover up her lady bits, because holy hell balls, his face was right there, but he swatted her hand away with a growl. He looked about as hungry as a man could get, and his eyes, which should've terrified her, couldn't pass for human. Shifters used to scare her, but now, a trill of excitement and anticipation zinged up her spine. Aaron hooked his arms around her legs and yanked her to the edge of the bed. In a moment of mortification, she closed her eyes, but then his lips touched her. Then his tongue touched her, so lightly, just a lick, and fuck every uncertainty, she suddenly wanted him to finish eating her more than she'd ever wanted anything.

With a moan, she slid her knees wider to give him more room, and reaching between her legs, ran her fingernails through his hair. When Aaron sucked gently on her clit, she arched her back, gasping at how good it felt. She was so close already, but he'd known that. This was the game, right? Get her close, then demolish her with his clever mouth and make an intimate memory she would never forget. One that would annihilate every experience she'd ever had in the bedroom before Aaron had plowed into her life.

"Oh, Aaron," she cried as his tongue plunged deeply inside her.

He wasn't claiming her skin, wasn't claiming with a bite. No, tonight he was claiming her soul.

The pleasure became blinding until a deep, throbbing orgasm blasted through her body. She'd never felt anything so consuming as the release at the urging of Aaron's mouth. In a flash, Aaron pulled her toward him until her ass was off the bed. There was a moment of imbalance, where she thought she might topple forward, but Aaron was there, holding her steady. He brushed the tip of his cock against her throbbing entrance. She didn't know where his briefs had gone but she gave zero fucks about that right now. All she wanted was to finish every aftershock she could with him buried deep inside of her.

Aaron snarled as he pushed into her. He rolled his eyes back and gritted out her name. His arms were flexed and looked hard as stone, his tattoos stark against his pale skin. An inch deeper, and he hit her sensitive nub. Her body gripped him over and over as he dipped deeply inside of her. Aaron shuddered, and she got it. She was right there with him, feeling high as a kite on endorphins.

When Aaron lifted his bright gaze to hers, there was some emotion there she couldn't understand. Something intense. "Don't give me your back," he growled out in a voice too low and gravelly.

"Why would I—oooh," she moaned as he pulled slowly out and pushed back inside of her. He was huge and stretched her past what she'd thought her body able to handle, but it felt so fucking good connecting to him like this.

Aaron lowered down and kissed her, his warm torso pressed deliciously tight against hers. His teeth grazed her bottom lip, and she repaid him in kind, biting his back. Angling his face the other way, he thrust his tongue against hers and pushed in again.

Too slow. He was going too slow, and already she felt the needy pull to beg him to pummel her. He was trying to be sweet maybe, to let her recover from her last orgasm. But as she clawed desperately at his back, she realized it was something else that had him taking his time. A feral snarl rattled up his throat, and his muscles twitched under her nails as he drove deeply into her. He dipped his mouth to her throat and clamped down, held her there for a moment before he released her and licked the tingling vampire bite.

Here was a man at war with his animal.

She should be scared, terrified, but instead a trill of lust crackled through her body. "I like this side of you," she whispered. Alana trailed kisses down his jaw, slightly dusted with raspy blond whiskers, to his neck. And then she played his game, clamped her teeth at the base of his neck and held him there as his animalistic sound vibrated against her lips. He pushed into her harder, held the back of her head, and curved his body around her, as if he was encouraging her to sink her teeth into him.

She could. Nothing was stopping her. It's not like she could Turn him into a human. It would just be a mark that told other woman to back the fuck off her man, and right now that sounded pretty damn good.

Could she tap into her animal side and actually bite him, though? Could she hurt him with her teeth?

Aaron drew out of her and thrust hard again. She was getting close to another orgasm. He drove her farther up the bed, spread his knees wider, and bucked against her again and again, harder and harder. His hand tightened at the back of her hair, and he rasped out a word that changed everything. "Please."

And she was lost to the moment, his hand pulling her to him, his dick swelling inside of her, every tensed muscle in his body curved around her in a way that begged her to bite him.

Closing her eyes, she clenched her jaw and pierced his skin.

"Harder," he demanded.

Clutching at his back as he pounded into her, she bit him as hard as she could. Warmth trickled into her mouth, but Aaron didn't even flinch in pain. Instead, he clutched her tighter as the sound in this throat rumbled through her mind, filling her senses. She released him and threw her head back as he slammed into her, faster, faster. Gone. She was gone. Every nerve in her body reached for him. His skin was too hot right now, but she didn't want to ever disengage. She would burn before she let him go.

Aaron let off a helpless noise as he slammed into her and froze. His shaft swelled and pulsed inside of her with the first shot of release, and her body reacted with the first explosive pulse of another orgasm. She screamed Aaron's name because nothing had felt like this, nothing in her life had been as big as this moment, as mind-blowing. Desperately, she moved her hips against his as pulse after pulse rocked her body. Aaron eased back by inches, then rammed her, shooting another hot jet of seed into her.

Now, she was hot on the inside, too. How could another person consume her like this? How could he make every cell in her body *feel* him? She was a matchstick and Aaron was fire.

Burying his face against her neck, Aaron twitched over and over, slower and slower until both of their aftershocks had faded away.

She thought he would pull away and disappear into the bathroom like the other men in her life had done, but instead Aaron lifted her up, straddled her on his lap, and just sat there on the edge of the bed, holding her. Rocking her. Smelling her neck. Rubbing her back right along her spine with such a gentle touch it made her want to cry for reasons she couldn't explain.

Moments ago, he'd been wild and barely in control, but now he was showing a tenderness she'd never seen in any man.

His shoulders were tense, so she cared for him, massaging them until he relaxed.

"I'm sorry," he murmured, successfully confusing the hell out of her.

Easing back, she said, "It's okay. That was…" Helpless, she shook her head. There wasn't a word big enough. Dipping her voice to a whisper, she murmured, "That was everything."

"I shouldn't have asked you to bite me."

His neck had bled freely, red trickling down and pooling in the bowl created by his collar bone.

The guilt settled in. "Does it hurt?"

"No, no, it's not that. I just wanted to take things as slow as you wanted."

An accidental smile stretched her lips.

"What?" he asked.

"You were successful, Aaron Keller. We took it as slow as I wanted, and apparently, I wanted to bite you." She made chomping sounds against his throat and then giggled when he tickled her waist.

"Swear," he demanded, but at least his voice was lighter now, less growly. "Swear you aren't mad at me for pushing us."

"So worried for nothing," she murmured. His eyes reflected strangely in the moonlight. "Silly beast, worrying about the feelings of your prey."

"No, Alana." Aaron ran his thumb reverently over the deep scar on her lip. When he pulled his hand back, blood was smeared on it. "You're the beast, and I'm your prey. My heart is yours. My bear, my life, everything. You can have it all. Just give me a chance to make you happy."

He was asking her to stay, and she already knew her answer. She'd known it from the moment she'd admitted to him how she wished she was stronger, and he'd deemed her good enough. Her heart felt bound to him in ways she'd never been able to fathom before it happened. This was the moment she'd always dreamed of—the moment when she belonged to another completely, and he belonged to her.

There would be no leaving Bryson City now. There would be no more planning a perfect future. There would only be building a new one here, with Aaron.

Alana sighed and slid her arms around his neck, rested her cheek against his shoulder, and kissed the claiming mark she'd given him. "Whether you Turn me or not, I'm yours, Aaron. I'm not going anywhere. As long as you want me to stay, I will."

"Always," he murmured, rocking her gently.

Dreamily, she asked, "Hmm?"

She could feel his smile against her cheek as he let his lips linger there. "I want you to stay for always."

Alana's eyes burned with emotion. What a beautiful offer that was. Having a man she cared for so completely asking her to put down roots deep and wide—to intertwine them with his own and start a future with him. Her life here wasn't ending as she'd been convinced it was. Aaron had come in and breathed brilliance into this place, made her see herself and her list of plans differently.

*Always.*

Alana smiled and hugged him closer.

Always was a good start.

# FOURTEEN

*Bam, bam, bam!*

Alana yelped and sat up in bed, scrambling with the sheet to keep her boobs covered. "What is happening?" She searched frantically for Aaron, but his side of the bed was empty.

When the muffled sound of laughter drifted through the log walls, she sighed with relief. The banging picked up again, and she blew a curl out of her face, then slid out of bed, dragging the entire sheet with her.

First, she peeked out the bedroom door to the living room and kitchen, but the house seemed to be empty. Alana shut the bedroom door and made her way to the bathroom as waves of masculine voices floated this way and that through the walls. She expected to be horrified when she looked in the mirror, but she was pleasantly surprised, likely due to the epic and thorough boinking Aaron had given her last night. Her hair was Texas-big but her curls had held, and her cheeks had a rosy tint to them. She didn't look exhausted like she did most mornings. Just happy.

What time was it?

She picked up Aaron's watch on the counter and gasped at how late it was. Ten o'clock? She'd practically slept all day! Thank goodness for her part-time employee, Marina, running the café on Fridays so Alana could have a day off to pick up her nieces from school and spend the evening in Asheville. Lissa had always been so protective and borderline judgmental. Alana had never dated a guy Lissa was pleased with. It was as if her twin sister had taken over the role of mom after their mother had passed. She was pretty sure Dad would be an easier sell on Aaron than Lissa would be, but okay. She would have to be brave and just lay it out on the line because she loved Aaron.

Loved Aaron?

Alana's reflection looked utterly shocked, and then she grinned. Yeah, that felt right. She loved him. Maybe it was fast for normal people, but Aaron was different. Their relationship was different.

"He's the one," she whispered, excitement nearly doubling her over as she tried to keep her happy squeal in her throat.

Lissa could get on board or not, but Alana was doing this. On second thought, though, maybe she wouldn't mention how she'd bitten Aaron last night. Lissa wouldn't understand it was special and not gross.

She readied for the day quickly so she could see Aaron sooner, and by the time she bounced out of the house and onto the saggy front porch, she was nearly humming from the inside out with anticipation.

"There she is," Ryder drawled from his place lying face down on an old plastic lawn lounger in the yard. He was wearing gym shorts and a smile and nothing else.

"Hey," Aaron said from the side of the cabin where he was holding up a dark green shutter next to the window while Weston drilled it in. Aaron's smile stretched across his entire face and landed in his blue eyes. He usually gelled his longer hair back, but today it was loose and falling in his face on once side, and he hadn't shaved this morning, so his jaw glistened with blond stubble. A white skin-tight sweater clung to his muscular torso, the sleeves rolled up to his elbows, exposing those tattoos she found so gosh-dang sexy. How had she ever thought they made him look like a bad boy? Aaron was a good man.

"I've got the rest of this one," Weston murmured around a couple of screws hanging out of his mouth.

Aaron pushed off the shutter and strode directly over to her, hopped up onto the porch, and squared up to her. With an easy smile that shook up the butterflies in her stomach, he leaned down and sipped at her lips until she melted against him. Resting his forehead on hers, he murmured, "Damn, it was hard not to wake you up."

"You missed me?"

His grin widened, and his cheeks turned a rosy color.

"Oh my gosh, are you blushing?" she asked.

Ryder made an offended sound in his throat.

"Aaron, hold on tighter! Don't let go of your man card."

Aaron shook his head and bit his bottom lip as his cheeks turned redder. And now the butterflies in her stomach turned to falcons as her own cheeks heated with pleasure. Big, burly tatted-up, feral shifter, and Aaron Keller was blushing for her?

"Next one," Weston said.

Aaron squeezed Alana's ass firmly, gave her a wink, and made his way to a pair of dark green shutters that were lying in the grass near 1010. When movement caught her eye, Alana looked up to see Wyatt pacing the road by the gate. His voice echoed through the clearing as he called, "Anything yet?"

"No, Wyatt!" Ryder yelled. "Queen Sky Lizard hasn't called us, and if she wanted you to know where she was, she would've sent you a memo." Ryder stretched his fingers for a small blue cooler that was just out of his reach and grunted. "Alana," he whined.

"Are you serious?" she asked, highly amused as he wiggled on his stomach closer to the edge of the white lounge chair.

"I'll be your best friend."

"Sorry, man," Aaron said, holding up another

shutter for Weston to screw in on the other side of the front window. "Her best friend card is full."

"Second best friend," Ryder amended. He reached half-heartedly again, wiggling his fingers pathetically. "Please," he rasped.

"Helpless man," she said through a giggle as she pulled a drink out of the cooler. "A canned margarita? Really?" Whose man card was in danger now?

"And that straw." Ryder pointed to a green swirly straw resting inside the cooler.

Alana shook her head, opened his margarita, and shoved the straw in, and all the while she lectured him. "Ryder, if you're trying to tan your pasty skin, maybe don't do it when it's forty degrees and cloudy."

He slurped out of the can and sighed like he'd been parched. "I saved a seat for you."

"Where?"

He moved his foot over a few inches. "Just there. On the corner. Second best friends only."

"Don't touch me with your feet."

He smiled sweetly around the swirly straw. With his freckles and muscles and bright red hair, she imagined he got whatever he wanted from the ladies. Usually men like him annoyed her, but Ryder was funny, so she pulled out a margarita of her own, shook the ice off the top lip, and sat on the corner of his lounger.

"We can share the straw if you want?" Ryder offered.

"Ew, no." She swatted his legs to make more room because her ass needed more than the four inches of space he'd made for her.

"Anything?" Wyatt asked from the gate.

Ryder thrashed around dramatically and pushed his torso off the lounger. "No, Wyatt! Harper's a fucking fire-breathing dragon, and she doesn't need to be coddled! She's probably in town getting you a two-month anniversary present or something else equally disgusting."

Wyatt went quiet, and Ryder settled back to slurp on his straw.

"Our two-month anniversary was last Friday," Wyatt called.

Ryder's eyes went dead. "I'm gonna kill him."

Aaron tossed Alana a grin over his shoulder as though he was as amused as she was.

When he let go of the shutter, it held. Wiping his dusty hands on his pants, he made his way to the back of a jacked-up truck with the tailgate down. There were piles of supplies inside, including yet another pair of green shutters. They didn't really go with the rustic cabin, though.

"What are you guys doing?" she asked.

"This is what it looks like when shifters go insane," Ryder explained.

"Not insane, just superstitious," Aaron murmured, pulling old rusty screws from the cheap plastic.

"When Weston had his first dream about you, he called home and asked for the shutters of an old trailer that got passed around the crews when we were growing up. And if that isn't crazy enough, we had to stop by the feed store in town to buy this." Ryder reached behind the lounger and picked up a small plastic cage filled with wood chips. Inside was a little black and white mouse dragging a giant nutsack.

Alana startled and moved to the edge of the seat when Ryder shoved the cage closer to her. "Are you going to eat him?" she cried.

"What? Why would I eat him?" Ryder asked. Realization spread across his face so fast his ears moved back. "Oh, because I'm an owl shifter?" He shook his head like he'd never been so disappointed in all his life. "I eat steak, Alana. Cooked steak." He shoved the mouse cage in her lap and plopped down. "My own second best friend…"

"I apologize for him," Weston said. "He was raised by animals."

Alana laughed and relaxed back onto the seat to better see the little mouse that was eating a pile of seeds in the cage. If she ignored the giant nards, he was pretty dang cute with his little pink ears and teeny tiny whiskers. "What's his name?"

"Sammy Scrotum."

"Dammit, Ryder," Weston growled from around the screws in his mouth. "I told you we aren't naming him Sammy Scrotum."

"Fine. Swampnuggets. Timmy Testes. Gary Gonads. Double Truffles. I mean come *on*, Weston, the little guy has an awesome set of 'em. It's like dragging a damn trophy everywhere he goes, and you're going to deprive him of a warrior's name?"

Alana pursed her lips against her laugh because Weston looked really annoyed at Ryder now.

"How about Alana picks the name?" Aaron said. "He's really for her, right?"

"Okay, I choose Sammy Scrotum, and what do you mean?"

Ryder pumped his fist at the name she chose and then explained, "The old trailer, ten-ten, was magic. It always had a resident mouse running around in it for as long as I could remember."

"But why are you doing this for me?"

"Because we want to keep you," Weston said. He locked his bright green gaze on hers and dared her to look away. "I'm superstitious because I know there are some things that are unexplainable. If there is a tiny fraction of a chance that the shutters from the old trailer and a mouse in the house can make you any safer, that's what's going to happen."

Okay then.

Aaron jerked his attention to the front of the property, and a moment later, Ryder and Weston swung their gazes that way, too. Wyatt was already pulling open the gate.

"She's baaaack," Ryder drawled softly, sitting up. "Wyatt's gonna be pissed."

"Why?" Alana asked.

Aaron came to stand beside Alana, hands on his hips as he sighed a troubled sound. "Because Harper ordered the three of us to stay put and keep Wyatt distracted so she could do something reckless."

"Reckless how?" Alana asked, but the boys had gone still and silent, watching grimly as the white diesel pickup truck bumped and bounced up the road toward them. Harper parked in the yard by Weston's truck, then got out slowly.

Her arm was covered in streams of red, but she didn't seem to favor it as she slammed the door. And when Harper swung her gaze to Alana, both of her eyes were glowing blue with elongated pupils. Alana hunched inward instinctively and clutched Sammy Scrotum's cage tightly to her stomach. Right now, something about Harper amped up her instinct to flee.

"What the fuck happened to you?" Wyatt asked, horror and fury tainting his voice as he brushed his finger down his mate's arm. The blood was dry.

"It's healed, let it be. Crew meeting."

Alana squeezed Aaron's hand and moved to excuse herself.

"Alana, you stay. You're part of this now." Harper approached slowly, lifted her chin, and then with a slow blink, looked at the bite Alana had made on

Aaron's neck. "Aaron, the vamps won't come after your mate again."

Aaron swallowed hard, his face angled away as he exposed his throat to his dragon-blooded alpha. "What did you do?"

"I went to Aric's house, and then I ripped the boards off his basement windows and let the sunlight in."

"Is he dead?" Aaron asked in a hard voice.

Harper sighed, but the breath was punctuated by a soft prehistoric rumble that lifted the fine hairs all over Alana's body. "No, he isn't dead. Singed yes, but not to ashes. There is still a part of me that wants to avoid a war with the vamps. I have a feeling we would lose lives on both sides, and I can't stomach the thought that I could've avoided that. This is his last warning, though. I recited the names and addresses of every member of the Asheville Coven to him and warned him that I *will* drag every fucking one of his vamps from their beds and into the sunlight if any one of us is harmed again."

"I had it handled," Aaron gritted out.

"It isn't your responsibility to handle it alone, Aaron. Look at your neck. Look at Wyatt's." Harper jammed a finger at the thick scarring on her mate's neck. "Mine." She gestured to faint scars on her own throat. "And now Alana's? Too many people in my crew have been bitten, and Aric's attack last night proved they aren't finished with their destruction. I'm fucking done giving those bloodsuckers chances to kill us. Things are changing as of now. We're shifters, born of some of the most powerful bloodlines in the world, and we've been rolling over trying to tiptoe down lines other supernaturals have drawn. This is where we draw our own line."

"How did you find their addresses?" Wyatt asked in a careful tone.

"I began tracking them the night after you killed the queen."

"Whoa," Ryder said, sounding impressed. "Damon Junior."

Harper's eyes flashed with anger. "My grandfather isn't here, and he has nothing to do with what happens to us. I'm not Damon Junior. I'm Harper of the Bloodrunners, and my patience in this matter is done. Any slight done to you by the vampires, you bring it to me. That's an order." Her voice shook with barely checked rage. "If a single...hair...is harmed on one of your heads, I will burn the Asheville Coven to nothing and devour their ashes."

Harper looked at each of them dead in the eye, then pushed past Weston and strode up the road toward the other cabins.

Weston and Wyatt's slow smiles matched as they watched her leave.

"Ooooh, she's gonna get 'em," Ryder said excitedly.

Alana expected to look up and find a troubled expression on Aaron's face at the reminder of a war with the coven, but there was another story written into his features. His chin held high, pride for his cousin sparked in his clear blue eyes.

Baffled, Alana whispered, "What just happened?"

"Harper's been tiptoeing around being alpha since she took on the crew," Weston murmured.

"Not anymore," Aaron said. "She just owned it."

Wyatt swung his bright-eyed gaze to Aaron and crossed his arms over his chest. Something significant passed between them in an instant, and Aaron nodded. "I guess it's time to decide who is Harper's Second. We owe it to her so she can feel settled."

"She doesn't care if it's you or me, man," Wyatt said low. "She just wants it done. Hell, I do, too. My bear is struggling with the pecking order here. I just want to know where I stand, but you've been half-assing the fights and nothing gets solved."

Aaron scratched the back of his head and let off an irritated growl. "Wyatt, it wasn't like I was trying to make this harder. I just got you back, man. I don't want things to change between us. The Breck Crew doesn't do this. Rank was already established by the time I came into it. I wasn't raised in the Ashe Crew, or the Boarlanders, or the Gray Backs. I'm not used to fighting a friend just to say my animal is more dominant."

Weston took his camouflage baseball cap off, then slid it over his dark hair backward. "Aaron, just get this shit done. Don't think. Just let your bear do the work so Wyatt can let go, too. Harper's owning alpha. One of you two needs to own Second so she doesn't feel alone at the top. If I had a bear, I would wreck you motherfuckers without a single thought about it. I don't, so I can't. Stop drawing this out. This isn't the Breck Crew or any other crew so stop comparing them. We're the Bloodrunners, and this shit needs to be hashed out before we can grow. Stop stunting us."

A muscle right under Aaron's eye jumped just before he pulled his sweater over his head. Alana was stunned at his rippling torso as he moved. Sure, she'd felt his rigid muscles last night in the dark, but seeing his bare torso in broad daylight had her ovaries doing a fireworks show. His pecs were chiseled, each abdominal muscle defined, and he had more tattoos over his ribs. His hair was mussed from undressing, and without meeting her eyes, he kicked out of his shoes as Wyatt stripped off his shirt.

"Come on inside with me, second best friend," Ryder said. "This ain't gonna be pretty."

"No," Aaron cut in. "She stays here." His eyes were that inhuman green-gold when he cast a quick glance her way. "Coddling you won't protect you, Alana. If you choose to be a part of this crew, you'll see all of it."

"It's okay," she murmured, trying to keep the worry out of her voice. "I've watched boxing before."

"This'll be a little different than that," Ryder said.

"What do you mean diff—"

A monstrous blond grizzly bear exploded from Aaron. He landed so hard on all fours, the ground tremored under her feet like an earthquake.

Alana had never seen an animal so massive. He had long, muscular legs and paws bigger than her head. Long, white claws curved out from the pads of his feet, and above his shoulders was a muscular hump that towered feet above her. When he curled his lips back, long, razor-sharp teeth gnashed at the chestnut bruin that had burst from Wyatt across the yard.

Wyatt paced, eyes full of fury locked on Aaron, but the blond bear didn't have his head in the fight. That much was clear from the slight flaring of his nose and the way he swung his attention directly to Alana.

"No, no, no," Weston murmured, stepping in front of her.

Ryder cut off her view of Aaron's terrifying bear and pushed her backward slowly. "Aaron...Bear...she isn't yours to mark yet. Not like this."

But she could hear him now, a growl that deepened with every step he took toward them.

Wyatt was pacing closer, his feral eyes swinging

from her to Aaron and back, as though his bear didn't know who to charge. Shit, shit, shit!

"Weston, should I run?"

"No, don't give him your back," Ryder said in a hard voice.

She remembered now. Aaron had given her the same warning when they were together last night. She hadn't understood it at the time, but he'd been telling her not to run from his animal. Not to give him her vulnerable side, or he wouldn't be able to help himself.

Weston was begging Aaron to leave her alone, and Ryder's hand was tight on her waist as he backed them toward the corner of the house. A deafening roar made her hunch her shoulders against the terrifying noise.

Weston barked out, "Ryder!"

Time slowed to a crawl as Ryder jumped gracefully, arching his back like he would flip, but his clothes slipped away and his form blurred into a white streak. Ryder's talons dug into her arm just as she saw him—Aaron. A massive raven ripped out of Weston in an instant, leaving her wide open to Aaron's charging bear. Bear, they'd called him, as though the animal was separate from Aaron. Alana opened her mouth and screamed as the monster bruin bore down on her with a speed that didn't make any sense. His golden eyes blazed with the promise of pain, and as she was launched upward, he reached her. Horrified, she jerked her legs up just as his mouth clamped around the air. The resounding *clack* of his powerful jaws vibrated through her skin as she went airborne. Ryder and Weston pumped their wings against the air, their claws digging through her sweater to the tender undersides of her arms.

Her stomach still felt as if it was on the ground, and she had the acute sensation of falling backward. She couldn't catch her breath as she rose higher and higher. Below, Wyatt charged Aaron, who was staring up at her through narrowed, determined eyes. Wyatt T-boned him, and the flurry of violence that ensued shocked the air back into her lungs. Alana gasped as the roaring of bears filled Harper's mountains. Wyatt was on top of Aaron, slashing and biting, hurting him. And then in a flash, it was Wyatt on defense as Aaron barreled him backward. The resounding slaps of their claws made it feel like it went on for hours instead of seconds.

The rattling roar of a dragon blasted through the mountains, like some T-rex from ancient times. And then Harper was there. She was massive, her deep green wings spreading across the clearing as she circled around the grizzly fight. She had long, ivory horns arching from the back of her head, spikes down her back and tail, and her eyes looked like they belonged in a snake. When she opened her mouth, Alana expected a roar, but all she heard instead was a distinctive clicking sound.

The bears were getting too close to 1010, battling and brawling so violently that the old cabin wouldn't be able to sustain a blow. Harper heaved a breath and blew a line of fire so hot Alana could feel the heat from up here above the canopy.

The flames burned blindingly bright for an instant, then shrank to nothing but a scorch mark in the yard. But it had been enough to draw the bears out of the fight and for them to take stock of where they were, because Aaron locked his legs against his backward movement as Wyatt went on the attack. The second Aaron's back legs hit that scorch mark, he roared and countered, spinning out of the way as though it had burned him. Wyatt's reaction was slower, and as he righted himself and turned, Aaron was right there, mouth clamped on his neck, throwing his head back and forth, ripping at the chestnut bear.

She was high in the air now. Though she wasn't afraid of heights, her life rested in the grip strength of an owl and a raven. If they dropped her from here, there would be no surviving the fall.

Aaron slammed Wyatt to the ground, then froze over him, teeth on his throat, and Harper rattled the woods with another roar. In an instant, Aaron slipped back into his human form and dropped to the dirt on his knees. And right before Alana was flown too far away from him, right before the thick winter woods swallowed up the clearing, Aaron looked up into the sky at her, clenched his fists on his thighs, opened his mouth, and bellowed a feral sound that was tainted with pain and regret.

# FIFTEEN

Alana couldn't get the vision of Aaron bellowing that scream of frustration out of her head. The heartbreak in his voice rattled around in her mind and wouldn't leave her. She'd gone back to talk to him about what he'd almost done to her, but by the time she and Ryder and Weston had returned to the yard of 1010, Aaron was in the wind. Harper had hugged her shoulders and told her he just needed some time, but Alana had seen the worry in the Bloodrunner alpha's eyes.

And now Alana was sitting here in her sister's house, hands around a cup of hot coffee, staring out the window at the raindrops streaming down the glass, and feeling like Aaron was out there somewhere convincing himself to pull away from her.

Down to her bones, she knew he wouldn't forgive himself for what he'd almost done to her.

She hated this. She'd always been a woman to tackle problems right away, not let them fester.

But maybe he was right to take some time. He was letting her wrap her head around all of this. Now was her time to decide for certain to commit to this strong, loyal, complicated shifter who wielded an out-of-control monster inside of him. Would it always be like this? Today, Aaron hadn't been stronger than Bear. He hadn't been able to protect her from himself. It had been so damn close she could still feel the ghost of his warm breath on her leg as he'd tried to rip into it.

Was he just desperate to satisfy his instinct to claim her? To Turn her and make her his completely? Or was he trying to hurt her? Would he have stopped after one bite, or would he have killed her if Weston and Ryder hadn't been there to pull her out of his reach?

She could still run from this. She could still give

up her lease on the coffee shop, give up her lease on her apartment, pack her things, and move anywhere. But the thought of leaving Aaron behind, giving up those moments that had been so potently joyous, dumped a sinking feeling deep in the pit of her stomach.

She was in too deep now to just pick up and leave without ripping an important piece of her heart out.

"Where are you today?" Lissa asked from where she stood scrubbing dishes in the sink.

She'd always asked that when Alana was daydreaming, so she answered as she had growing up. "A million miles away from here." Alana frowned at the front door. "Where's Todd tonight? He's usually home from work by now."

Lissa looked a lot like Alana but a few inches taller, twenty pounds thinner, and with nary a scar on her pretty face. But today, her eyes were clouded with sadness. "He's probably just running late. I think he's taking me to that new Italian restaurant tonight."

Lissa's three little girls came blasting around the corner of the living room, through the kitchen and to the dining room, screaming and laughing as the oldest, Harley, chased the other two with a plastic snake.

Lissa told them to, "Stay outta my kitchen until I'm done cleaning it!"

And after they yelled, "Okay, mommy," from the other room where they were making destructive sounds, Lissa smiled at the plate she was scrubbing.

"Little monsters, but I don't know what I would do without them." She cast Alana a strange look, as if she was considering a question, then shook her head and went back to washing.

"What?"

Lissa blew a dark curl out of her face and said, "Remember when we were about to graduate college, Todd and I were about to get married, we were planning the wedding, and you'd organized that bridal luncheon?"

"Yeah, I was the best maid of honor you could've ever asked for."

Lissa snorted and nodded. "Truth. But remember when we were all sitting around the table and the girls were asking me when Todd and I would start having babies, and then they talked about how many they wanted, and you got real quiet?"

Alana ducked her gaze and spun her coffee mug slowly in her hands. "I didn't get totally quiet. I answered."

"You said you didn't ever want babies, and the others teased you and didn't take you seriously, but I knew you meant it. And I knew why."

Alana bit her bottom lip to punish herself for the emotional burning in her eyes. Lissa never allowed conversations like this. Not real ones. Not anymore, and damn it felt good to just connect with her again. But this was painful. "I didn't want babies because the cleft palate is genetic. Mom had it really bad, so did I, and I didn't like myself very much at the time we were talking about it. I was about to mess up all your wedding photos. I didn't want my babies to feel like that ever. I remember every time you got 3D ultrasounds when you were pregnant with the girls, I would just kind of dread it and hold my breath through your pregnancy until their faces came back perfect. I just didn't want them going through the surgeries like I had and still look like this." Alana gestured to the deep scar on her lip—the one people still stared at.

"Do you still feel the same about having

children?" Lissa asked carefully.

Alana thought about it for a minute, then patted the other side of the table. "I want to talk to you about something."

"Something bad?" Lissa asked.

"No. Just something I need my sister on."

Lissa wiped her hands on a dish towel, poured herself a cup from the steaming coffee pot, and sat across from Alana. "Lay it on me."

"I met a guy."

Lissa's perfectly shaped eyebrows raised. "Wow. Okay, do I know him? Does he live in Bryson City, or is he one of the guys you met online?"

"Uhhh, he's new to the area, a fire fighter for the Bryson City Fire Department."

"So he's the guy you mentioned the other day on the phone? Not the online one, but the other one?"

"Yes, but there's more. You remember how I had that huge crush on one of the shifter cubs when they first came out to the public?"

Lissa laughed and nodded once. "How could I forget? You were so annoying about him. It was all you would talk about at dinner, what he'd been photographed doing, what the paper said about him.

You spent all your allowance on those teeny-bopper magazines that featured his pictures. Adrien or Allen..."

"Aaron Keller."

"Yeah, that was him."

Alana pursed her lips and waited for Lissa to put it all together.

Her sister's face went comically blank. "Wait, you're dating Aaron Keller?"

Alana giggled at the shocked tone in Lissa's voice. "I am. And I really like him, but his life is...complicated."

"Alana, he's a fucking shifter."

"Mom said fucking!" Harley sang from the other room.

With a mom growl, Lissa leaned forward. "What the hell are you thinking, Alana? They're dangerous. Do you not remember Shane?"

"He was a werewolf, and you dated him for three weeks."

"And he was awful. He wasn't right in the head. I could see it in his eyes. They were empty. He said all the right things, but meant none of them. He was way too rough. He was terrifying, Alana."

"And he was a werewolf," she repeated through gritted teeth.

"What's the difference? He's a shifter! Your children won't just be at risk of having a cleft palate, Alana. They will have an *animal* inside of them."

"Can you just let your guard down and listen to me for a few minutes? Save your judgement because it will only make me shut down, and I really, really need to talk to someone about this. Someone who isn't part of his crew and doesn't have some stake in this."

Lissa looked pissed, but at least she stopped herself from saying so by sipping her coffee and glaring over the rim.

"He makes me feel good."

"Well, they are notorious for being rutting beasts, so of course the sex is memorable."

"That's not what I'm talking about. He makes me happy. I can't keep my eyes off his firehouse down the street from my shop when he's on shift. I can't help but worry for him when he's out on a call. I get giggly and giddy when he shows up in my café, and when he touches my lower back, or hugs me, or kisses me, I feel happy. I mean really happy. Like the kind that changes your life and makes you see the world differently." The fire lessened in Lissa's dark eyes, so Alana pushed on. "He's not what I imagined for myself when we made that stupid list in college, and he doesn't meet all the requirements, but I'm starting to think he was meant to come into my life and shake things up. Like he was meant to make me feel alive and whole and destroy my preconceived notion of the perfect man. He isn't perfect. He's got tattoos all over his body, and piercings, and he's a shifter. But he's also caring, loyal, strong, and respectful of me and proud to bring me into his crew. And last night I…" She should stop now, but a sudden urge to share everything with Lissa like they had done when they were kids washed through her. "I bit him."

"Bit…him?"

"Yes. I gave him a claiming mark because it felt right and my heart was in it, and he feels really big, Lissa. Really important. He feels like my future. And I don't think he will be able to let me stay human if I choose him. He has a problem with his animal and wants to Turn me. He wants to claim me. And it's terrifying, but at the same time, it's thrilling that the man I love wants me to be his so badly he can't help himself around me. I didn't find him early like you did. Year after year I waited for Prince Charming to come because that's what everyone said would happen. 'You'll meet someone who's just right for you, Alana. When the time comes, you'll find your man.' And here I am, thirty, no kids, at a crossroads, having accepted that I'll never have what you do, and Aaron walks into my life and turns everything upside down. I don't know what to do, Lissa. Do I leave Bryson City like I'd planned and give up something that could be amazing because I'm afraid? Or do I stay and see this thing through?"

Lissa huffed a breath and sank back in her chair, crossed her arms. She blinked hard and shook her head like she was disappointed, but then she uttered a combination of words that shattered Alana's view of everything. "Todd and I are separated."

"What?"

Lissa licked her bottom lip, checked the open doorway to the living room, and lowered her voice. "For the last year, he's been living in an apartment a couple blocks away."

Horrified, Alana asked, "Why didn't you tell me? I

mean…" Holy shit, what? "I've been coming here, picking up the kids from school so you could get date nights together. Lissa, why didn't you tell me?" she repeated louder.

"Because then it would be real! I didn't tell anyone. Not you or dad. We haven't told Todd's mom either. The girls don't know what to make of it, but we're trying really hard to make our marriage work."

"Are you getting divorced?"

"No." Lissa winced. "I don't know. Maybe. We're trying really hard to hold onto each other, but somewhere along the way, he fell out of love with me. As hurt as I was the first time he told me that, I feel the same now. We're in it for the girls right now."

"So, your date nights?"

"Sometimes we go out and try to rekindle things, and sometimes he doesn't feel like working on it and I go to a movie by myself. We meet up at the end of the night for the show. He's still devoted to co-parenting the girls."

Shocked, Alana ran her shaking hand over her forehead. "Shit, Lissa."

"I know. It's a mess, but it's my mess."

"No, it shouldn't only be on you. Look, I know

you're tough, but sharing the stuff you struggle with doesn't make you weak, Lissa. You aren't my mother. You're my sister, and I wish you would've let me in. I wish you would've let me hug you and listen to you and not feel like such a damned outsider in your life."

"The point in me telling you... I don't ever remember feeling what you described with Aaron about Todd. I don't remember that passionate, heart-pounding lust, love, infatuation, excitement you described. I liked him, we were compatible in bed, and we were good at conversation. When we graduated college, we were supposed to get married, have kids, and live happily ever after because that's what people did. Those were the logical steps. And I felt so lucky because my life was perfect. But now, looking back, I wish I had waited for someone who made my heart race. And I think Todd is missing that, too. So...okay, Aaron's a shifter. If he makes you happy, maybe you should give him a chance and stay in Bryson City. See where your life can go. Maybe it'll be scary and overwhelming." Lissa leaned forward and lowered her voice to a whisper. "But maybe being with him will be the greatest adventure of your life."

Alana released a relieved breath and reached across the table, clutched onto her sister's hands. Lissa would never know how much her acceptance meant to her because Alana didn't have the ability to fully put it into words right now. Not when she was choked up like this. But as Lissa's eyes filled with tears, Alana thought maybe she understood anyway.

"Fuck Todd, and fuck date night," Alana murmured. "Get him over here to watch the kids and let's go out to a movie, just you and me."

Lissa smiled emotionally. "Really?"

"Hell, yeah. We'll go drinking afterwards, cut loose. Be wild for a night like we used to and forget all the stress. What do you say?"

Lissa nodded, brought Alana's hands to her cheek, and rested them there. And after a moment, she sniffed and nodded. "I'd really, really like that."

# SIXTEEN

"I can't believe I did that," Aaron muttered for the tenth time since this afternoon.

Ryder popped the top of a beer and handed it to him, then sank into the rocking chair beside him with a sigh. "Relationships aren't easy, but I'm telling you, don't count Alana out yet." Ryder took a long swig of his beer and stretched one leg out, rocked the chair under him gently. "She's tough, man. I sensed it from day one, and so did Wes."

Aaron clicked his tongue against his teeth and shook his head. "Wes was fucking right with that dream of his."

"Okay, but let's dissect that dream. Nobody knows how his visions work in the first place, and even if it was a hundred percent accurate, he dreamed of her staring right at you, tears in her eyes. She wasn't running away screaming." Ryder's ruddy brows arched up like point-for-me. "Besides, I was with her after you tried to bite her. She was sprinting back here after she saw you go human again." Ryder leveled him with a look. "Sprinting. She was worried you were hurt from the fight, but you'd already taken off."

"Because I wasn't okay to be around her yet—"

"But you need to get there, Aaron. Alana's classy. Way too good for your dumb ass, and she isn't going to put up with running for long. She won't. If your animal needs work with control, get your shit handled. Work on it. Make him good enough for her because, yeah, someday, Bear could be her maker, and it'll be up to you to make that transition as easy on her as possible. But putting her under an out-of-control animal?" Ryder shook his head and took another gulp of his beer. "Weston and I won't always be there to save your ass."

Weston appeared out of the shadows in a pair of

black sweat pants, his hair disheveled. "Couldn't sleep," he murmured.

He'd been having trouble with insomnia lately, but the Novak Raven wasn't fooling any of them. He was avoiding the visions. Weston sat down on the porch floorboards of 1010 and rested his back against the rail. He had a long piece of grass between his fingers, and he began shredding it with a troubled look on his face. "Has she called you back yet?"

Aaron stared at the dark woods beyond the porch light and shook his head. He'd been holding his phone the whole damn night in hopes that she would return any of his three calls. He didn't know where she was, but he had made sure Aric was on shift tonight, so at least she was safe from him. Still, he didn't like this sick feeling that he'd ruined everything, and that's why she wasn't answering his calls. "I think I messed it up."

"You didn't," Ryder murmured.

"But it feels like I did. Down in my gut, it feels like she really saw me, and it scared her off. I can't get it out of my head—that look on her face when I was coming for her." Aaron swallowed hard and picked at the label on his bottle. "I had zero control. I was trying so fucking hard to stop Bear. Or, for fuck's sake, to even slow him down enough so you guys could get her out of my reach. And her eyes were so big, just terrified. I could see my own reflection in them, bloodlust written all over my face, jaws open, and I couldn't stop myself. I gave the animal my skin, and what was his reaction? He wanted to bite her more than anything. My animal wants her claimed so she won't leave me. I hope you two never feel what it's like to terrify your mate."

"No chance of that," Weston said low. "Ravens don't form bonds like bears do."

"Bullshiiiit," Ryder said. "Your mom fell for Beaston when they were kids, and she never let him go. I can't wait to terrify my mate. In the bedroom." He pitched his voice high. "Oh Ryder, your dick is so big!"

Aaron chuckled and took the first long sip of his cold drink. Talking to the guys had always made him feel better. He could use the distraction right now as he clutched his phone, hoping every second that Alana would offer him salvation and call him back.

"There he is," Ryder said as Wyatt appeared out of the dark. "Third in the crew, how does it feel?"

"Better than fourth and fifth." Wyatt jabbed at the bird shifters as he sat on the porch across from Weston.

Ryder pulled his beer bottle to his mouth like a microphone. "Wyatt James, you grew up with everyone saying you would be a great alpha someday. How does it feel to lose alpha to a girl, and then Second to a rival bear shifter?"

"Fuck you, man," Wyatt drawled, but he was smiling, and some of the tension that had been hurting Aaron's chest eased.

"So we're okay?" Aaron asked, trying to keep the hope from his voice.

"Yeah, brother," Wyatt said, and his voice rang with honesty. "I didn't care either way, second or third. I just wanted Harper to be able to settle. Maybe I thought I would be alpha when everyone was feeding me that line growing up, but things don't always work out like we think when we were kids. None of us imagined we would be in North Carolina, so far from Damon's Mountains, or linked up in a crew together. We didn't think we'd be under Harper. But I'm happy with how things turned out. My bear feels good since the fight. Controlled. Relieved maybe,

I don't know. Plus, I don't have to make any of the hard decisions. I can just be the muscle." Wyatt reached over and slapped Aaron's boot. "We're good."

Aaron let off a gusty exhale, expelling some of the pressure off his shoulders that had settled onto him after the fight.

"Where's Harper?" Weston asked.

Wyatt stretched his legs out beside Weston's and rested his hands around the railing behind his head. "Sleeping like a normal person. She doesn't stay up all night like we do. She has a crew of dipshits to run."

Ryder tipped up his beer in a silent toast. "Fair point."

Wyatt got a faraway look in his steady blue eyes. "Remember when Aaron spent the summers with us in the trailer parks, and we would all sneak out to that treehouse Beaston built for us?"

Ryder chuckled and rocked back in his chair. "Yeah that was super fun until you got caught fooling around with Harper and all of our parents went into lock-down mode. I shit you not, my mom put a security system in our trailer, not to keep robbers out, but to keep me in. I couldn't lift up my windows without the alarms going off."

"I remember the first time you tried!" Aaron said. "You woke up the whole trailer park. I was staying with you, remember? Your parents woke up pissed. Your sisters, too."

"We hauled ass out of there, and Dad was yelling through the window, 'Boy, you better get back here before I ground your ass into adulthood.'"

"God," Aaron mused. "I've never been so terrified in all my life. Your dad's a beast, man. When he made threats, it was so hard not to listen to him. But you were running like your tail feathers were on fire, and I didn't want to turn around and face him alone. Ryder, you were such a hellion. I don't know how he put up with you."

Ryder scoffed. "I was a perfect angel. Until I got my flight feathers."

"Yeah exactly," Aaron said, smiling before he took another sip of his beer. "I always looked forward to summers up there because the photographers weren't stupid enough to come into Damon's territory. Summers meant no school, late nights, shifting whenever I wanted, finding trouble with you guys, and no one was hiding in the bushes trying to get pictures of me."

"Please, those magazine spreads got horny shifter groupies swooning at your feet," Wyatt muttered. "You didn't hate all of it."

"Speaking of..." Aaron leaned forward and rested his elbows on his knees. "Alana has a poster of me. She showed it to me the other day."

"Whaaat?" Ryder asked, his eyes sparking with faux-shock in the porchlight. "Aaron Keller paired up with a fan?"

When Aaron's phone chirped in his hand, he jerked, nearly spilling his beer in an effort to check the new message. He read it twice, trying to understand it.

*Went to movie and saw furry bear.* There was a picture attached of a blurry grizzly bear on a movie screen. And then it was followed by another blurred image of Alana's perfect cleavage peeking out of a V-neck sweater.

*Boopsie, didn't mean to send last one. Haaa! I didn't get arrested. You aren't supposed to take pictures in a movie theater but I'm mated to a mother fuckin' BEAR. With tattoos. I got in trouble. I'm bad to the bone.*

Huh.

*I'm sorry about earlier*, he typed, because that should be the first thing she heard from him. Send.

*Me too. I told my sister everything. She knows how big your dick is.*

Aaron grinned and ran his hand down his two-day facial scruff before he responded. *Are you drinking?* Send.

*No, I'm done drunk. Dead drunk. Drunk as a skunk. What does that even mean? Do skunks drink? Wanna fool around on the phone?*

Another immediate picture of her cleavage came through, this one a bit clearer, but behind her, there was a crowd of people.

*Are you in a bar? Fooling around in there probably wouldn't work.* Send.

*Frisky. My sister says hi. I can go into the bathroom? There are three stalls.*

He laughed and shook his head. What was happening right now? *Woman, I'm not having phone sex with you while you are in a bar bathroom.* Send. *Where are you? Do you need a ride home?* Send.

*Taking a cab home. With my sister. Lissa loves me! We're having so much fun.*

*Good.* Send. *Soooo...are you mad at me?* Send.

He waited, but his phone stayed silent, and his glowing screen faded to black.

"Is her sister hot?" Ryder asked from where he was leaned over like he'd been reading the conversation from beside him.

"She's Alana's twin, so probably."

"Twins?" Ryder balled his fist at his crotch and flung his fingers out while he made an exploding sound.

"God, I feel sorry for your future mate," Weston said to Ryder, but the raven shifter was trying and failing to hide a grin.

Aaron settled back in the chair and muttered, "Talons off, perv. Alana's sister is married."

"Is Alana mad about you almost biting her?" Wyatt asked carefully.

"Right now she sounds hammered, but I'm sure when she wakes up tomorrow she'll remember what I did."

"Mm," Wyatt grunted, rocking upward. He dusted the seat of his jeans and meandered off toward his cabin in the woods. "Night."

"Night," they all murmured in unison.

Weston followed with a small wave, and Ryder

chugged the last gulp of his beer and stood. Aaron thought he would give him the mannish handshake they always did, but instead Ryder shoved him in the head and told him, "Don't fuck this up."

Ryder jogged down the porch stairs and into the night, and Aaron was left staring at the blank screen on his phone, his last question bouncing around in his head. *Are you mad at me?*

She might be tipsy, but Alana wasn't ready to let him off the hook yet, and he didn't blame her.

He was pissed at Bear, too.

# SEVENTEEN

Alana's head felt like she'd squished it into a motorcycle helmet three sizes too small. She had a pulse right behind her eyes that sizzled with pain every couple of seconds.

The Senior Seven were happy, their mugs full, their plates only half empty as they chattered about some almost-B&E that had been detailed on Bradford's police scanner this morning. The culprit was Daryl Sanders, though, and he was a lover of the whiskey and likely just tried to get into the wrong house again. It had happened before. The handful of other customers in the café were either cleaning up to leave or just sitting down at a table with the pastries they'd purchased. It had been surprisingly busy today, and normally, she would've loved the extra business, but she was nursing one hell of a hangover right now. Alana hadn't been that liberal with the Lemon Drop shots since she was in college.

Her phone made the pretty three-note chord that said she had a message. She was hopeful it was Aaron, but the noise made her wince.

It was from Lissa.

*I had so much fun last night. I really needed that, sis. Not just cutting loose, but actually talking to you about real stuff. I love you bunches.*

Alana grinned and typed in, *Love you too, Lis.*

The bell over the door rang, and when she looked up, a pair of familiar, powerful, jean-clad legs strode in. She could make out the bottom hem of Aaron's black sweater sitting on his tapered waist just right, but his torso and face were completely blocked from her view by a giant vase of bright pink roses.

"What is this?" she asked as Aaron settled them on the counter with a lopsided grin.

"An apology."

Pleasure warmed her cheeks as she plucked a tiny present from the center of the arrangement. After opening the small box, she pulled a packet of painkillers from it and gave him a questioning frown.

He gave her a charming wink that successfully leveled her ovaries to nothing. "For hangovers."

She giggled. "I actually really need these today."

Sitting in the bottom of the box was a small picture of Aaron's bare chest, abs, and the top of his jeans, which he'd left unbuttoned. She could just make out the top part of his dick. Alana nearly choked on air. She clutched it to her chest, scanning the room as if she just got busted reading a naughty book in public.

"That's repayment for those tit-tease pics you sent me last night," Aaron said through a cocky grin.

Yeah, she kind of remembered that. She'd have to go back and read everything she'd messaged him now that she was sober. Now she was staring at the picture, and Aaron chuckled in a way that said he was sexy and he knew it, so Alana rushed to shove it in her back pocket.

"You don't like it?"

Alana snorted. "Please. I'm gonna blow it up and

make a new poster of Aaron Keller for my adult self."

"Hang it right above your bed, yeah?"

Alana pressed her palms against her cheek to cool the heat there. "Stop."

"Will you go out with me tonight?" Aaron asked suddenly. He opened his mouth like he wanted to say more, but changed his mind and left that question to fill the space between them.

"You like me," she murmured.

With a grin that deepened his smile lines and made his bright blue eyes dance, he admitted, "I fuckin' *like* you."

Alana couldn't help the excitement that bubbled up her spine and made her take a few running steps in place. One of her curls bounced out of her pins and fell in front of her face. Aaron cast a quick glance behind him, then brushed it back and tucked it behind her ear. "Say yes. Go out with me. Let me make up for what I did."

The smile dipped from her lips. "Aaron, you don't have to keep apologizing for that. I understand."

He lowered his voice to a whisper. "I feel like shit about it."

"Buy me a slice of pizza from that Italian

restaurant down the street, and I'll forgive you."

"The one you went to on your date with Doucheface?" Aaron's lips thinned to a line of displeasure.

"Yeah, there are, like, ten restaurants in this town, and I don't want that one associated with Trey the Troll." She ducked her gaze and admitted, "I want everything here soaked in the memories I make with you."

Aaron took a step back like he'd been pushed. His eyes had gone round, his face angled in question. "What are you saying?"

Alana sighed and wrung her hands on the counter. "You didn't scare me off, Aaron. I called this morning and extended the lease here."

"Are you serious?"

Why was she so emotional about this? Blowing out a shaking breath, Alana nodded.

Aaron strode around the counter so fast she gasped, and his body crashed against hers in a lung squeezing hug. He lifted her off the ground and carried her into the kitchen and out of view of the curious café patrons. Aaron just stood there and held her as his heartrate went wild. "Fuck, fuck, fuck," he said too growly. "You aren't teasing me? You're staying in Bryson City? For sure? Officially?"

She laughed thickly and hugged his neck tight, buried her face against his shoulder. "For sure and officially. I thought about it a lot, but I can't leave this place. I can't leave you. It would be like leaving a piece of myself behind. I don't know what you did to me. I should be scared of you after yesterday, but all I wanted to do was see you again and tell you it would be okay. And I wanted you to tell me it'll be okay. That you aren't running either."

"I'm not running, Alana." He kissed her neck twice and whispered it again like an oath. "I'm not running."

"Okay, then pizza tonight."

"And then what? Woman, I know you have plans."

She giggled as he settled her on her feet and looked down at her with eyes that had darkened two shades. "And then you'll take me on another date, and another, and when you're ready, you're gonna ask me to marry you. You're gonna respect my human side. Someday, I want your last name on me."

Aaron cupped her neck and kissed her lips

gently. And when he eased back, there wasn't an ounce of hesitancy in his eyes as he murmured, "And then what?"

She gripped his wrists so he wouldn't let her go, wouldn't let her fall. "And then you'll mark me and make me like you. You'll do it right, and we'll prove Weston's dream wrong. And your bear will settle because he'll finally understand, without a shadow of a doubt, that I'm not going anywhere."

And she wouldn't. This was the moment she owned a future with Aaron. Lissa had been right. This was the adventure, throwing caution to the wind, and trusting her heart. Her head still had moments of weakness, moments where she got scared of the pain and uncertainty that would flow in and out of this life she was choosing. But what could she do? Her soul had wrapped around Aaron long ago.

No matter what came their way, she was ready. She wasn't facing the world alone anymore—not since Aaron had walked into her life. Now she felt like an important half of something bigger than she'd thought love could be.

A couple weeks ago, she would've balked at the unpredictability of a future like this. She would've clung to her lists, her plans, and her safe life if it had been anyone else other than Aaron. But her mate had come in and made her feel *alive*.

Aaron's eyes were clear and sure as he looked at her as though she was the most beautiful woman he'd ever seen.

Now, the unpredictability wasn't so scary anymore—not with Aaron right here, so steady and strong against her. Even after yesterday and how close he'd come to Turning her, she still somehow felt safe in his arms.

She would take a life of uncertainty with Aaron over a half-life of constancy without him any day.

# EIGHTEEN

"I need to get up there and change those lightbulbs," Aaron said, squinting down the street from Dante's to her lit-up Alana's Coffee & Sweets sign. Half the letters were out, and the C was flickering on its last legs. Right now it read, *Alan's Cof & Swet.* Appealing.

"How are you going to reach it?" Alana asked, setting down the empty wine glass. The table had been cleared half an hour ago, but she and Aaron had just been enjoying the night. It was cold out on the front patio, but the manager had turned on the giant heater right behind her so she was plenty comfortable.

Aaron's gaze turned thoughtful. "I bet Chief would let me use one of the big ladders.

She swatted his arm. "Quit looking at it like that."

"Like what?"

"Like it's an ugly sign. That's my baby."

"It's a hideous baby."

"Neat freak," she muttered, crossing her arms over her chest. "You know, I had all these plans for the café."

"Oh yeah? Paint me a picture."

"Imagine this," she said in a theatrical voice. "Out front, a handcrafted wooden sign stained a rich walnut color. New windows without BB gun holes that have been patched with putty."

Aaron chuckled and nodded. "I like it already. What else?"

"I wanted wood floors. Not the new ones, but the refurbished old, scuffed-up kind. I wanted chandeliers, proper wainscoting, and designer paint. Better tables, nicer mugs, and eventually I wanted to upgrade my oven to a double so I could get my baking done faster. And I always wanted to get Wi-Fi set up so people could work in there."

"It sounds awesome. What's stopping you?"

"Money. You've been in there. The place isn't exactly hopping. Even during the busiest months, I barely cover the cost of running the place and my bills. I drained my savings to start up the business, and there just isn't money left over for the big stuff."

Aaron frowned, and then his troubled gaze was back on her sign again. Ready to move away from her failures with the café, she asked carefully, "Do you want to see a picture of me as a baby?"

As if Aaron could tell how big a deal this was to her, he pulled her legs onto his lap under the table and gave her one of her favorite smiles. The one where his lips curved up higher on one side. "Yeah. I really do."

Nervously, she flipped through the pictures on her phone to one Dad had sent her and Lissa a couple months ago when he was going through old boxes of pictures. The caption read, *my beautiful baby girls*.

Sometimes she forgot how bad her cleft lip and palate had been, so when the picture had come through in the message, she'd sat there shocked for several minutes before she was able to respond back to him.

There it was. Alana zoomed in to crop out the crib she and Lissa had been lying in. Lissa was looking up with her big, beautiful eyes, lips formed in a sweet coo, and Alana had a big grin on her face as if Dad was playing peek-a-boo over the side of the crib.

Her smile was wrecked, her lip split all the way up through the left side of her nose, and part of her palate was missing.

With a steadying breath, Alana handed Aaron the phone over the small table. He stroked her calf gently as he pulled the phone to him. She didn't want to see his face when he saw her deformity for the first time, but for some reason, she couldn't look away.

The smile dipped from his lips for just an instant but didn't leave his eyes. He zoomed in farther, probably on her, and murmured, "Alana, you have the same smile. You're so fucking cute."

"Don't say that. It took a lot of money to make my smile different."

When Aaron poked the screen a few times, Alana frowned. "What are you doing?"

"Sending this to myself. I'll get my mom to send me some baby pics of me so I can give them to you."

"Y-you want to keep that?"

"Hell yeah, babe." He looked at her as if she'd lost her mind with that question. "Nothing about your journey here turns me off. I love your lips, scar and all. Let me ask you something." He leaned back in the chair and pushed her phone away. "Do you think you would be the woman you are today if you weren't born with the cleft lip and palate?"

Well, that shocked her into silence. She hadn't ever thought about that before. Would she be this self-assured, or proud of herself for getting through what she had? Would she know she was this resilient if she hadn't been teased and overcome it? "No, I don't think I would be who I am."

Aaron angled his face and his smile was back, genuine and proud. "Well, I *love* the woman you are. I'm sorry for what it must have cost you when you were a kid, but I don't think we would be here now if you hadn't pushed through it. That scar on your lip means I got a shot to keep you. It's one of my favorite things about you."

Alana blew out a shaking breath and blinked back the moisture that was rimming her eyes. She would not ruin this beautiful moment with mascara streaks and relieved sobbing. No one in her life had been able to help her love her scar, but Aaron just had with a few sentences.

He looked so handsome here in the soft strands of outdoor lights that wrapped the pergola above them. His hair was pushed back on top, his eyes so blue and honest, his smile lines bracketing his sensual lips. He hadn't shaved this morning or yesterday, and the gold stubble on his chiseled jaw made her fingertips itch to touch it. He wore a charcoal gray and black striped sweater with a V in the neck that gave her a peek at the defined line between his pecs and a hint of the tattoo that curved along his collarbone. His sleeves were pushed up to his elbows, exposing more ink, and his long legs were clad in dark jeans. He'd admitted when he picked her up tonight he had dressed up for her, and she loved that. This right here felt like the most important date of her life, and now his words had erupted her stomach with a fluttering sensation.

Alana pulled Aaron's paperclip from deep within her pocket and spun it slowly in her fingertips. "I know what this means," she whispered. "Harper told me about you giving a paperclip to your dad when you first met him, and about how he kept it. She told me you kept this one all this time." She swallowed hard. "And then you gave it to me."

Aaron's hand on her legs had gone still under the table as she'd spoken, and he looked uncertain, but he needn't be.

"You have this amazing ability to pick your people at first sight," she said thickly. "You did it with your dad, and then you did it with me. And I just wanted to say I love you back." That last part tumbled from her lips quickly so she wouldn't change her mind and chicken out.

Aaron froze, and his blue eyes morphed to that unsettling muddy gold color that seemed to glow unnaturally. There he was—Bear. He should be here listening to her declaration too.

"I love both of you," she said on a breath.

Slowly, Aaron leaned forward and plucked the paperclip from her fingertips. He settled his hands under the table in his lap where she couldn't see and stared at the trinket with such a thoughtful look in his blazing eyes.

Aaron adjusted his weight and pulled something out of his own pocket. It was a small tube of something. Hesitating only a moment, he handed it to her.

"What's this?" she asked, fingering the tiny treasure that had been warmed in his pocket.

"That's the burn cream you gave me the first time I met you."

Her face went slack with realization, and she dragged her gaze back to the medicine in her palm. Her voice quaked when she asked, "You kept it?"

Aaron nodded, but he wasn't looking at her anymore. He was fidgeting with the paperclip. And when he finally gave her his bright-eyed gaze, his face was full of some emotion she didn't understand. He lowered her legs out of his lap and onto the ground, and for a moment, Alana was scared she'd angered him. She was scared he was pushing her away again.

But instead, Aaron pulled her chair closer, leaned forward, kissed her lips, and then pulled away with a gentle smacking sound. Something cold touched her fingertip, and she looked down. It was the paperclip, smoothed out and re-shaped to wrap around and around in a perfect circle. Aaron had slid it up to the first knuckle on her ring finger.

"Oh, my gosh," she whispered.

"Alana, I don't have the ring you deserve right

now, but I'll get it. You told me earlier that when I was ready, I would ask you to marry me, and it was so damn hard not to drop to my knee right then and there. I know what I want. I knew what I wanted the second I saw you, and with every moment I spend with you, my body...my heart...my soul tethers to you more tightly. You were right about the meaning behind this paperclip. I love you *so much*." Aaron slid off the edge of his chair and lowered to one knee.

Alana's shoulders shook with emotion as she held her hand over her mouth to keep her sobbing inside.

"Alana Warren, you are the most beautiful, tender-hearted, funny, patient, forgiving, strongest woman I've ever met. And I'd be honored...*honored*...if you would be my wife. Will you marry me?"

Her emphatic nod dislodged the moisture in her eyes so that tears streamed down her face as she croaked out her answer, "Yes."

Aaron's smile was instant, relieved. He pushed the paperclip ring onto her finger, then pulled her to him and hugged her tight as though he never wanted to let go.

A few couples sitting at tables around them began clapping and whistling. Alana laughed and held him. Feeling overwhelmed with emotion, she stared up at the strands of lights, mirroring the stars in the dark sky above. She'd forgotten they weren't alone here because Aaron had that uncanny ability to make her feel like they were the only ones in the world.

Or perhaps it was more.

Perhaps it was that Aaron made her feel like the only one in *his* world.

Alana clenched her left hand to feel the texture of his paperclip on her finger. She'd waited her whole life for Aaron, waited her whole life for this moment, and he'd gone and made it so beautiful.

No matter what came now, they would face life together. She wasn't alone anymore.

Now and always, she would remember this as the night when her life truly began.

# NINETEEN

Alana sipped her glass of red wine and settled it back onto the uneven floorboards of 1010. She wrapped the blanket Aaron had draped around her shoulders tightly around herself and stretched her leg out across the open doorframe she leaned against. This had become her favorite part of the evenings when Aaron wasn't on shift at the firehouse.

Over the past two weeks, November had drifted into December, and the second snow of the season was here. It wasn't common to have the frosty stuff on the ground in these parts, but it sure painted a pretty picture.

She'd always hated the snow and ice down in Bryson City where life would grind to a halt, but up here in Harper's Mountains, she'd never seen the woods so beautiful.

The rhythmic *chop, chop* of Aaron's ax cutting through firewood on the chopping block relaxed her. She was bundled up to her chin, but Aaron was out in front of the cabin working in nothing more than a pair of jeans and a T-shirt, as if the cold weather didn't bother him at all. Would she be immune to cold someday when she was Turned into a bear?

Alana rested her cheek against the doorframe as she watched him shove off a split log and settle another one on the block. His cheeks were red from the chill or the exertion, she didn't know, but when he cast her a glance, as he so often did on nights when they were just content to be like this, his eyes were steady and blue, and Bear was nowhere near the surface.

Bear had been easier for Aaron to manage lately. She spun the paperclip ring around and around her finger out of habit. Something about Aaron's proposal had made his animal more manageable. He still wouldn't risk Changing around her and only did it when she was working at the coffee shop, but someday they would get there. Someday he would completely trust himself around her.

Outside the golden halo of porch light, a giant snowy owl and a black raven flew by low to the ground. Their powerful beating wings kicked up the snow in little tornadoes as they passed.

Aaron looked up at them, nodded his chin in greeting, and Alana waved. The boys were probably in for the night since it was late and the storm was supposed to get worse.

Alana would've loved a snow day inside with her mate, but he was on shift tomorrow first thing. Aaron loved his job and was passionate about it, but he'd recently started telling her how much the hard stuff affected him, affected Bear. Now she prayed every time he left their bed for a shift at the firehouse with his gear bag in hand that today he wouldn't lose anyone. That he and the fire crew would get to whatever crisis fast enough to help.

She could always tell the shifts that had been hard because he would come into her coffee shop the morning after work with ghosts in his eyes. He wouldn't talk, and she didn't need him to. He would take her back to the office and just hold her for a while until the soft snarl in his chest faded to nothing.

At least he wasn't shouldering this alone anymore. At least she could offer some reprieve.

So much had happened in the last two weeks. Aaron had met Lissa and Dad, and Alana had video-chatted twice with Aaron's parents, Cody and Rory, and even his two younger sisters who still lived in Breckenridge with the Breck Crew. Rory had cried a lot when Alana showed them the paperclip ring. She wasn't in a rush to replace it with a big sparkly one. This one meant so much to her.

She'd kept the lease on her coffee shop, but not on her apartment. She'd made the repairs from Aric's attack and moved her stuff up to 1010. Why? Because nights didn't feel right if she wasn't with Aaron. Even when he was on a shift and couldn't sleep beside her, 1010 still felt strangely like home. Maybe it was her growing friendship with Harper and the boys, or maybe it was the call of these mountains that had etched themselves so thoroughly into her heart. Maybe it was the little black and white mouse that ducked in and out of view that kept her loneliness at bay. Or maybe Weston was right, and there was something magical about this place. She believed in that stuff now, fate, all of it. What else could explain making it to this moment, filled with infinite happiness, watching Aaron Keller, the boy she'd adored in her youth and loved today, chop wood for the fire that would keep her warm all night?

She'd thought moments like these hadn't been meant for someone like her, but she'd been wrong. She'd just had to stop looking to find it.

Aaron gathered split logs into his arms and strode up the stairs, dusted the snow off on the welcome mat before he stepped over her. She smiled up at him, then at the boot prints in the snow that led directly to her. The clatter of the logs being dumped next to the fireplace in the bedroom sounded, so she drank down the last couple sips of her wine. She knew what was coming next.

Aaron came back to her, hesitated over her with a tender expression on his face, then dipped and picked her up like she weighed nothing. He nudged the front door closed with his boot, carried her into the bedroom, and then settled her onto the bed, blanket and all.

Propping the pillow under her cheek, she

watched as he made the fire in the small stone hearth. And when it was crackling and glowing and the first wave of warmth washed over her skin, she asked the same thing she did every day like this. "Are you happy?"

"You already know the answer to that," he murmured in that deep timbre of his.

"I like to hear you say it."

Aaron locked his arms on either side of her shoulders on the bed, trapped her in his gaze. "I've never been so happy." The mattress creaked as he leaned down and kissed the answering grin from her lips.

Alana slid her hands down his stomach and hooked her fingers in the waist of his jeans. His skin was warm under her touch, but it wasn't enough. Slowly, she pulled his shirt over his head, let it slip from her fingers onto the floor, then admired his body as it tensed with the soft breaths he took. His hair was mussed from taking off his shirt, so she ran her fingers through it to mess it up more. She loved when he looked disheveled.

Aaron grabbed her wrist, kissed it, then slid his palm up her hand and linked their fingers. He kissed her knuckles gently and asked, "How did I get so lucky?"

She didn't know the answer, but she knew how he felt. As she stared at their linked hands, his skin shades paler than hers, she felt like the lucky one, too. She'd never known what to expect in the man she would finally settle down with, but Aaron had turned out to be her perfect match.

He released her and pulled the blanket off, then her shirt and pajama pants hit the ground, too. He was gentle and took his time, kissing her skin that he had exposed while she melted slowly into a puddle of wanting. His teeth grazed her neck where the bite mark from Aric had healed to faint scars. Writhing against him, she let off a needy sound and rolled her hips up at him seductively. *Take me.*

Aaron's lips collided with hers, and a snarl rattled up his throat as he ground his hips against hers. He worked his biting kisses down her throat and then drew her nipple into his mouth. He sucked hard enough until she could feel his teeth, so she hissed and grabbed his hair. That only seemed to spur him on, though, because his fingers dug deeply into her hip.

Since he'd almost bitten her, Aaron had bedded her gently, but this was different. This was him letting her glimpse his animal side. This was rutting dominance and passion and uncontrollable desire, and she loved every fucking second of it. The rip of his zipper rivaled the growl that rattled his chest, and Alana spread her legs wider, inviting him closer.

She thought he would take her deep and hard, but he cupped her sex and slid his finger into her instead. "I like how wet you always get for me," he murmured, and when she looked up again, his eyes were blazing a bright glittering gold.

"Bear," she whispered.

Another snarl, louder this time, and Aaron pulled his hand away and pushed his long, thick shaft into her.

Arching back helplessly, clutching the sheets in her clenched fists, Alana cried out at the pang of ecstasy that pumped through her body just with that one thrust. And then he was in it if the feral sound in his throat was anything to go by, completely lost to the grinding of their bodies. She'd never witnessed him wild like this. Never felt him rough like this, but it meant he was letting her really see him. Really letting her in.

He leaned down, clamped his teeth on her neck, and then released her. *Yes, yes, yes!* The grin he flashed her when he pulled away was nothing shy of wicked, the tease.

He slammed into her, harder now, his stomach flexing every time he filled her. His arm locked behind her back, he pushed in deeper, hit her clit perfectly at the peak of every roll of his hips.

"Fuck, Aaron, yes! Harder!"

Aaron gritted his teeth and pulled out of her, spun her on the bed so fast it stole her breath. *Never give me your back.* Oh, she was about to get herself bitten by her mate, but for the life of her, she couldn't conjure a single, solitary fuck. He grabbed her ass and pulled her backward. He shoved his palm against the small of her back, making her arch for him, and then he gripped her hair as he pushed his swollen cock inside her. Alana gasped out a helpless sound as he pulled back and pounded into her again. Her arms shook with how good her body felt right now. With the force of him bucking, she fell forward onto her elbows, spread her knees wider, and groaned as he pushed deeper. His arm wrapped around her middle, gripping her breast as he picked up his pace, harder and faster. Pressure, pressure, so much pressure. It was building too fast, too blindingly hot in her middle as he filled her over and over again. As the first throbbing sensation of her orgasm exploded through her, Aaron's chest rested onto her back. Clamping his teeth onto her shoulder blade, Aaron froze, his dick swelling and pulsing inside of her as jets of hot seed flooded into her.

Aaron drew out and pushed in again, every muscle in his body tense against her. Again and again, he throbbed inside of her until she rocked with him numbly, completely high on release.

Her mate left her skin unbroken, then rested his forehead on her back as he exhaled a long, shaking breath. His body twitched against her once more before he pulled her over with him and hugged her back to his chest. His kisses gentled, right over the place he'd thought about biting her. And oh, she knew he'd considered it. He'd tempted himself with it, but he'd been strong enough to resist.

She turned in his arms, completely exhausted and sated, and pressed against him. Her breasts were so soft in contrast with his rock-hard body. And when she looked up at him, his eyes were still as gold as fire, but he wore a slight smile.

She could almost feel his pride—could almost feel the relief wafting from his skin.

"Good Bear," she whispered.

Aaron turned slightly, and the glow of the fire behind him reflected off a mark she'd never noticed before. There was a dark patch in the shape of a strawberry on his neck. She'd thought she had memorized everything about his body, but it was on the side Aric had ripped up when the Bloodrunners had killed the Queen of the Asheville Coven. Naturally, because it looked painful and made her hate the vampires, Alana's gaze just skipped right over the scarring there so she'd missed this little treasure.

With a frown, she sat up and traced the outer edge of the mark. "What is that?"

Aaron propped his cheek on his arm and rolled his eyes closed as though her petting felt good. "It's a birthmark. All the men in my family have them." He grew quiet for a while, just content to let her trace the darker skin, but finally he murmured, "That was how my dad knew I was his the first time he saw me."

"Do you remember the first time you met him?"

His lips twitched into a pained line, then softened. "Yeah. I was five, and I know memories that old are supposed to fade, but I still remember it like it was a few minutes ago. It's one of my brightest memories. I started Changing when I was one, and I was a brawler. Raised by just my mom, who was human at the time and had no clue my dad was a shifter. She didn't even know they existed until I turned into a little bear cub. I didn't have any control at all. I still remember how it was. I would fight the Change, and when I did, it would slow it down. I would just cry and cry as my bones broke one by one, and when I got my canines in, my mom had to protect herself from me. She had to put me in a cage when I had to Change."

"Oh, my gosh, Aaron."

He made a dismissive ticking sound, then opened his bright gold eyes. "She did the best she could. I hurt her really bad once. Clawed her down her entire forearm, and I remember watching her cry and bleed, but I was still on the attack. Bear was a monster from birth. Or maybe the human in me was too weak, I don't know. My mom took me to Breckenridge to meet my dad and beg his help because I was getting too big, too out of control, and she hated caging me. It made me worse. Made me wild. Made me feel crazy for days afterward. I remember my dad turned white as a sheet when he saw my birthmark. Just...no blood in his face, eyes changing to a color just like mine. It was as if my bear recognized him. I didn't know what it meant, but I felt...relief. I wasn't alone anymore."

"Did he work with you?"

"Yeah. He took me out in the woods and watched over me. It was the first time I could remember Changing outside of the cage, so I just went crazy. Running everywhere, sniffing everything. The woods were kind of like the biggest playground you can ever imagine. And he kept me out of trouble. When he brought me to my mom, I attacked her. Couldn't help it. Couldn't control it, but my dad swatted me hard. Showed me it hurt when I used my claws on skin. Reminded me of who she was, and it changed a lot for me after that."

"But not everything."

Aaron shook his head slowly and rolled onto his back, pulled her hand onto his chest. "I got better, but I never got control over my bear like I should've."

"Do your parents know?"

A nod. "My dad does, but not my mom. It would hurt her and make her feel guilty. My dad thinks those years Changing in the cage made my bear too wild. Too big. It gave him a chance to overpower what I could control because I stayed scared when I was locked up. I stayed hurt and trapped, and I was just a kid. It stifled my human side, so when Bear wants to take over, I still have a hard time staying present."

"But you did tonight. I gave you my back, and you didn't bite me."

The smile that spread across his face was slow and easy. In a whisper, he said, "That's why what we did just now is such a big deal. I was still here with you. I could stop him."

"You loooove me," she sang as she tickled his ribs.

He laughed and sat up in a blur, taking her with him. He settled her over his lap and kissed her, held her wrists so she wouldn't tickle him anymore. Little distractor.

And slowly, he released her and slid his arms around her back, hugged her tightly against his chest.

Burying his face into her neck, he inhaled deeply, as though he was committing her scent to memory. "I love when you smell like me."

"You or Bear?"

"Both." He sucked on her neck. "Bite or no bite, you're mine, Alana."

She eased back and traced the healed claiming mark she'd given him. It shone silver here in the flickering glow of the firelight. She thought of her poster of him, and of how she'd followed him as he'd grown up. Of how she felt that bone-deep connection before they'd even met.

Alana kissed his lips softly, then murmured, "Bite or no bite, you were *always* mine."

# TWENTY

*"Aaron."*

"Mmm," he murmured through the thick layers of sleep.

*"Aaron?"*

Aaron opened his eyes in the dark, his ears prickling as he listened. Alana's arm was draped over his waist, completely limp like she was still asleep.

*"Aaron, wake up."* It was Alana's voice.

He sat up quickly and stared down at her. It was hard to tell in the dark, but her lashes looked like they were resting on her cheeks.

*"Bite me. I'm ready."*

A snarl rattled his throat, and his instincts blared. He froze with the feeling that something invisible and terrifying was in the room with them. For a moment he was in the cage again, but the bars slipped away just as fast as they'd appeared.

*"Bite me, Aaron. I'm ready,"* Alana repeated again, her words tumbling over each other, repeating in quick succession.

Aaron shook his head hard to dislodge the remnants of whatever dream was fucking with him.

*"Aaron."*

"Stop it."

*"Please. Please do it now. I'm ready."*

He clutched his head. "I said stop it!"

Alana startled beside him, rested her hand on his leg. "What's wrong?" Her voice sounded...different.

"Help me!" Harper screamed from outside.

Aaron scrambled from the tangled bedsheets. "Did you hear that?"

"Yes," Alana said in a horrified voice. "Was that Harper?"

"Shit. Stay here." Aaron didn't bother with clothes, just bolted for the door.

"I don't want to stay here." Alana's voice rang

248

with a hollowness he couldn't understand.

Maybe she was right, though. He couldn't leave her unprotected. He pulled her hand behind him and bolted out onto the front porch. It was then that the woods rattled with a dragon's roar, and the night sky was blocked out by something massive. Harper's fire blasted down into the trees some distance away, and the glow lit up the dark night. The smoke was choking, but Aaron pulled Alana behind him and sprinted for the woods.

"What's happening?" Alana asked.

"War," he said. His body felt strange, as if it was being called into the battle.

"Aaron, hurry!" Ryder yelled in a frantic voice.

He pushed his legs harder, faster, and Alana ran behind him, spurred on by the fear he could smell wafting from her skin. Ahead, the stars were blocked out by bats. Mother fucking vampires. Aaron ripped a limb off a tree and splintered it in half, handed the sharpest one to Alana. "Don't let them near your throat."

Fuck, he didn't want to bring her any closer to whatever was happening in the woods, but a pained scream from up ahead froze his blood. No time. No time at all to hide her somewhere safe. They would come for her if he left her unprotected.

Up ahead, another wall of flame illuminated the woods. He could see them now. Wyatt's bear was clawing and biting viciously at the swarming bats, and Weston and Ryder were fighting human, armed with sharpened wooden stakes. Fighting thick purple smog. Fighting vamps they couldn't get their hands on.

The bats flew around Weston and Ryder and then up into the sky above them. Aaron could see it coming, and as horror spread its black tendrils through his body, he tried to scream out—tried to warn then. The massive cloud of bats circled above like a giant fist slamming down.

"Come on!" Weston screamed into the abyss as he bunched his muscles to fight.

He disappeared in the smoke.

"Weston!" Alana screamed.

Much closer than Aaron, Ryder was running for him. "No, don't!" Aaron yelled as Ryder disappeared into the smog. He had to help them, had to reach them. Had to save them from the hell they were in.

Twin screams of pain lifted the hair on his body,

and like a vacuum, the smoke and bats fanned from the woods. Weston was on the ground, not moving. And when Aaron skidded to a stop near where Ryder sat hunched over, Weston's eyes stared vacantly up at him, already dimming from the lack of life.

"No," Alana murmured in a broken voice. "Where's Harper. Harper!" she screamed as she fell to her knees and cradled Weston's head in her lap. Alana sobbed Harper's name over and over as if the Bloodrunner Dragon could bring Weston back to life.

Ryder's shoulders shook, and his lungs rattled when he inhaled. He was twitching oddly, and just as he fell backward, Aaron caught him. Blood poured from the side of Ryder's lips. Aaron wanted to retch when he saw the gaping wound in his stomach. "My b-brother. Blood brother."

"No, no, no, shhhh," Aaron said rocking him. "It's gonna be okay."

"Avenge my brother." Ryder looked over at Weston's blank stare and huffed a pained breath. And then he went limp in Aaron's arms, his eyes locked on the Novak Raven.

"Ryder," Aaron choked out, his eyes blurring with tears. "Ryder, please don't go."

Alana was doubled over in pain, keening and wailing, tears staining her cheeks as she looked to Aaron to do something.

Stunned with the deep agony that was ripping his heart open, he turned to where Wyatt had been fighting. He was nothing but a pile of matted fur. Aaron listened over the breeze for the sound of a heartbeat, a breath, anything. Nothing but dead silence filled his head.

The blood chilling *squeak-squeak* of bats sounded louder and louder, and above, the night went dark. Not a single low-lying storm cloud showed through the thick vampire smog. Aaron looked over in horror at Alana, and he knew she could see it in his face. He'd failed. Failed to protect his crew, and now he was going to fail to protect her.

He'd pledged his life to save her, and now they were out in the woods without a crew and too many enemies. It was all he could do to tackle her and cover her with his body when the bats reached them. He could feel them—the scrabbling fingers and claws of cold, dead hands.

"Hold on baby," he said as pain slashed at his back. The vampires yanked at her, and Alana's weight shifted out from under him with such power, he could barely hold onto her arms.

"Aaron, help me!" she screeched, terror punching out every syllable.

He couldn't see anything but her forearms and face in the thick purple smoke, and immovable hands were pulling hard on his body, prying him and Alana apart. He needed to Change. Needed to let Bear have his body so he could save her, but he couldn't let go or she would be in the air where he couldn't reach her. She was helpless, no weapons, no defenses. His feet made deep rivets in the snow where the vampires were dragging Alana, stretching her between them, hurting her.

Tears streamed down her face. "Please, Aaron...don't let them kill me."

In one last move of utter desperation, he yanked himself forward and sank his teeth deep into her arm. He bit down until blood streamed into his mouth. Until she howled in pain. Until he scraped bone with his canines because he had to make sure to give her the bear.

There was the claiming mark Bear had wanted to give her so badly.

*Please let this work. Please let her be a fast first-time Changer.*

Alana screamed as her hands ripped from his grasp.

And then she was gone.

# TWENTY-ONE

Alana dropped to her knees, and pain shot up her leg as she landed hard on a rock. She wanted to wince and remove herself from the ache. She wanted to run because she could still feel those cold claws scrabbling at her skin. But she couldn't move. Those vampires had been cowards, never showing their faces, killing the people she loved with no honor.

Aaron sat on his knees, clutching a branch in his lap, staring off into the woods as though he'd just lost everything. And he had. Weston and Ryder were limp beside each other. Wyatt lay unbreathing and alone on the edge of the tree line. Harper was gone.

Why had they dropped Alana? They'd had her, and she was what they wanted, right? She'd been the target in town, and they'd worked to pry her from Aaron's desperate grip. So why wasn't she airborne right now?

Power pulsed inside of her, and she closed her eyes as pain rippled through her like an earthquake. Gasping for focus, just so she wouldn't disintegrate with the agony in her middle, she clenched her fists. It was so hard. What was happening to her?

*The bear.*

Warmth ran down her forearm in a stream and dripped from her knuckles. *Pit pat, pit pat.* It felt like fire where Aaron's teeth had ripped into her. A fire that was spreading through every cell with terrifying speed. She was dying.

*Aaron.* She tried to say his name as the fear pulsed against her chest. *Help.* Those bats would be back. She grunted in pain as another wave of bone-deep pain ripped through her. Something was inside of her, growing, pushing against her skin, against her soul. She wasn't alone in this body anymore. *Aaron.*

It took a monumental effort to turn her face toward her mate. He was so close, right beside her, but he wasn't looking directly at her. Unblinking, he was looking at her cheek. What was wrong with him?

It was then that she saw it—her reflection in his eyes. She was staring up at him, terror written into every facet of her face, tears streaming down her cheeks, and her eyes...they were blazing gold, just like Aaron's. Just like her maker.

Weston's dream had come to fruition.

It wasn't just her that she saw there, though. Someone stood behind her. Someone in the shadows, just a smudge she couldn't make out. Fear trilled up her spine as she noticed something else.

Aaron's pupils were dilated so big his eyes were almost black.

Aric.

Alana blinked hard and forced her eyes to Ryder and Weston's corpses. This wasn't real. It wasn't. She blinked hard, and a soft snarl vibrated up her throat. Ryder and Weston's bodies flickered like an old lightbulb about to burn out, then solidified again. With a grunt, she narrowed her eyes. "This isn't real," she choked out.

Ryder and Weston disappeared from the woods completely, and when she looked over at where

Wyatt had died, he wasn't there either. There was nothing here but quiet woods. No death, no blood save her own.

"A life for a life," a familiar voice said from behind her. The snow crunched as Aric stepped around her. She could see everything now. Every shadow the moon cast, every leaf, every whisker on Aric's unshaven chin. Another growl rattled her chest.

"This is bullshit," a man said from the tree line, and then she could see them, too. There were others. Eight of them, at least. "The rules say we have to avenge our queen. How the fuck does having a human Turned into a shifter satisfy the Rule of Vengeance?"

"Her humanity was stolen, forced by our hands, and now we don't have to go to war," Aric said in a voice that ended in a terrifying hiss.

"I want him," the man said, stepping forward, his long nail jammed at Aaron. "If you can't make the proper decisions for our coven, Aric, I will. The bear dies. Look at his neck. You've already marked him for death anyway. Give him to us, and we'll leave this place satisfied."

Alana was shaking now, completely out of control of her body as something deep within her pushed to escape. "Touch him," she snarled in a voice she didn't recognize, "and I'll fucking kill you."

"Oh, she believes that," the man said, laughter in his tone.

"Raif," Aric warned as the man paced closer.

"Aric, did you hear the honest notes in her voice? Look around, sweetheart!" he yelled at her. "It's you and your brainless boyfriend, out in the deep woods and at our mercy. No one is coming for you. Your crew is fast asleep in their beds with Aric's soothing visions dancing in their heads."

A soft growl sounded from Aaron as Raif stepped closer, but his eyes stayed vacant. *Wake up, Aaron!*

Aric stepped in front of her, blocking her view from the dark-eyed vamp who wanted Aaron's neck.

"I am King of the Asheville Coven, and this is my ruling."

"It's not how Arabella would've done—"

"I'm not Arabella!" Aric yelled, his words snapping with power. "Have you forgotten what she did to our coven? She dragged us through the mud. She tainted everything we stood for."

"And what are you doing, Aric? Letting the Bloodrunner Dragon live, letting her mate live, letting her entire fucking crew live. You're a vampire!"

"Who believes in the preservation of life."

"Weak!"

"Smart, and you better fucking stand down Raif, or I will pluck your head from your shoulders, and we'll just see if it grows back. It's not like the old days when we could kill and get away with it. There are laws now, ours and humans, to contend with. I'm trying to protect this coven from any more loss. I'm trying to protect us from war. The Rule of Vengeance is satisfied. Her Change was forced. Listen to that growl in her throat. Listen! She isn't human anymore."

A long feral hiss sounded from Raif. Alana should be terrified right now. She should be plotting ways to run and drag Aaron with her, but something deep inside of her thirsted for blood and revenge. It thirsted to step in front of Aaron and protect her mate instead of giving these assholes her back. And that something was a snarling beast who wasn't afraid of anything. She gripped tighter to the sharp, splintered branch Aaron had given to her. He held one, too, but he wasn't breaking free from Aric's hold on him. Not like she was.

It must be the new bear in her middle and the need to Change. She wanted to retch at the wave of pain that blasted through her. Fucking Aric. He was keeping her from Turning.

Bats exploded into the air, and in an instant, she was released from Aric's mental talons. The second she could move, she reacted on instinct, adrenaline and rage in its purest form. This body was powerful, and so fast. She could see him, Raif, in the middle of the bats. There was a soft blue outline she hadn't been able to see when she was human, but the bear had different vision. Just as Raif stretched his claws out for Aaron, she pulled her mate out of his reach, then braced her feet against the snowy ground and blasted upward on tensed muscles. The limb made a sick, slick sound as it slid through Raif's ribcage and into his heart. His mouth twisted in a screech of pain as she snarled, "Told you I'd fucking kill you." Raif ignited into flames and exploded into trails of sparks and ash. She released him as the burn touched her palm, and as he hit the ground, he disintegrated to nothing but a Raif-shaped pile of ruin.

Chaos broke loose, but this body was faster now. She could see things coming and react just in time.

Bats, smoke, the sound of their fury, the roar of the wind they kicked up. Standing protectively over Aaron, she gave the beast her body. With a monstrous snarl in her throat, Alana charged Aric and ripped his arm backward just as smoke trailed from his body as he tried to escape. Too slow, and Alana needed him to let go of whatever hold he had over the Bloodrunners. She thrashed her neck, clamping her teeth as hard as she could onto his forearm. Aric grunted in pain, she could hear the effect of Aric's distress. He'd lost his grip on Aaron's mind, because the soft growl in her mate's chest turned feral, and the instant popping of bones echoed through the dark woods. The night echoed with his roar, and then he was with her, biting, slashing, maiming. Aric ripped away from her jaws, and from his body, bats exploded, flapping in a sickening, squeaking cloud toward the tree line. Back to back, she and Aaron fought as vampires dove at them and then away again in a constant, calculated attack.

Behind them, Harper's roar shook the earth. Now they'd done it.

They'd awoken the dragon.

Pain slashed across Alana's back and neck, but

she and Aaron just had to hang on a few more seconds. Help was coming. She could hear the beating of Harper's wings, could feel the furious wind she created. Another grizzly bellowed a battle cry, and a giant snowy owl dove into the smoke, followed by a massive raven.

The sickening slice of their corpse claws slashed into the skin of her back. Harper blocked out the sky and lit up the woods with a long line of dragon's fire. One of the vamps shrieked in pain, and there were less of them now. Less bats, less smoke, less neon blue shadows ducking in and out of the fight.

Out of the corner of her eye, she could see the vamp coming. Alana turned and hooked her powerful claws around the back of his head, slammed him down on the ground. She hated this creature. Hated him with every fiber of her being because they'd come here to Harper's mountains to hurt her, and to hurt the man she loved. They'd made her think Ryder, Weston, Wyatt, and Harper were dead. They'd forced her to hold Weston's body and watch Ryder's last breath.

Her dark fur was smattered with mud and blood, and her six-inch claws raked across the vampire's face as he struggled and screamed under her. She could smell it now, gas, and when the sound of a firestarter echoed above her, Alana clamped her teeth around the vampire's neck and threw him skyward. She watched in satisfaction as Harper blasted a ball of fire onto him.

And now they were fleeing—bats and smoke filtering through the woods like a storm cloud being drawn away from them. Harper chased them, lighting up the woods as she beat her wings furiously over the top of them.

Alana paced, unable to follow them because she couldn't leave Aaron. She didn't know why she couldn't put distance between them. She wanted to chase the vampires, to kill every last one of them, but she was tethered by something invisible to the dark blond bruin behind her.

"Alana," Ryder said in a soothing voice from a low branch in a tree. He was sitting there, naked as the day he was born, his legs dangling over the edge and a look of worry furrowing his ruddy eyebrows.

For some reason, her name on his lips in that tone pissed her off. She would not settle down right now. Those vamps had almost taken everything from her. Ryder hadn't seen what she had. She'd watched him die! Just the memory of Aric's death vision nearly doubled her over in agony.

Unable to control her emotions in this new body, Alana inhaled and roared at Ryder, then turned on Aaron. His animal was massive, a few feet taller than hers at his hump, and her paws sank into his titan prints in the snow. He backed up slowly, his bright gold eyes locked on her. She wouldn't hurt him, though. He was hers, didn't he know? *Mine. My mate, my Aaron. Mine to protect.* She'd come so close to watching that asshole Raif kill him. She wanted to squat on his disgusting ashes, but needed to touch Aaron more right now. With a heartbroken sound deep in her throat, Alana ran her head down the side of his jaw and came to a halt at his shoulder, buried her face there so she could block out the rest of the world. So she could remind herself he was warm and still breathing.

He smelled of fur and Aaron, and when he rested his chin across her back, she wanted to cry, but didn't know how to in this body. And then the pain was back, as if imagining her human form had brought the end to her Change. This one was slower and hurt badly. Her bones broke, her muscles reshaped, and when at last she lay panting in the snow, every inch of her skin felt like it had been ripped from her body.

Alana looked up at the clouds above, at the snow falling down. She hoped it covered Raif's ashes completely so Harper's woods wouldn't be tainted. Her skin prickled with cold.

And then Aaron—her Aaron—was there. "Baby," he murmured, wrapping her up in his arms. No longer were his pupils blown out, but he had long claw marks down the side of his face. More scars. He'd told her once scars were a part of this life, and there was no use trying to hide them. He'd said they were a reminder of what happened and what was to come.

Shivering, she looked down at her forearm at the deep, ragged bite-mark that had already sealed up. There was that shifter healing. She was Changed. It had happened so fast she couldn't wrap her head around the fact that, just moments ago, she'd been a massive, battling bear.

"You saved us," Aaron said, rocking her. "I couldn't get him out of my head, but you did. You saved us."

Ryder was there, and Wyatt and Weston now, too, kneeling around her as Aaron lifted her off the ground and into his lap. How was he so warm?

"My body hurts."

"The first Change is the worst," Weston murmured.

"Your dream came true," Alana squeaked out through her tightening vocal chords.

He searched her eyes, then nodded. "Yeah. I'm sorry."

Her smile dislodged a warm tear from the corner of her eye. "I'm not."

Harper landed hard between the trees and shrank into her human form, her eyes wide and on Wyatt. "Is everyone okay?"

Murmured confirmations filled the night, and Aaron helped Alana to stand. Her body felt like she'd pulled every muscle, but as Harper approached, her bear knew just what to do. Squeezing Aaron's hand for support, Alana dropped slowly to her knees in front of the Bloodrunner Dragon. Her body shaking with cold and shock and adrenaline, Alana looked up into Harper's mismatched eyes and smiled emotionally. She swallowed hard and angled her head, exposing her neck.

And then Alana whispered the word that would secure her place in the Bloodrunner Crew. "Alpha."

# TWENTY-TWO

"Are you sure I'm ready for this?" Alana asked, staring out the window as the snowy woods blurred by.

Aaron reached over the cab of his old winter truck and steadied her hand. Alana stopped twisting her ring. It felt different after Aaron had paid a jeweler to coat the paperclip in white gold. It was the same shape, but thicker, and with a smooth texture now.

"You're safe," Aaron promised her.

And he was right. Aric had quit the Bryson City Fire Department, and he and his coven had evacuated

Asheville. They were in the wind, but Aric had left a note in Aaron's locker at the station. Alana had read it so many times she had it memorized.

*I'm sorry. I hope you'll tell Alana that. This was the only way I could keep us all alive. I won't be seeking vengeance for Raif, and hope that you can convince your Bloodrunner Dragon not to hunt my coven. By the time you read this, we will be long gone. Please try to understand I really was just trying to lead my people out of the hole the queen before me had dug. You'll never see us again. Take good care of your mate, Bloodrunner.*

*A.*

The vampires were out of the territory, and Alana didn't have to worry about being controlled, hunted, or Turned. It was a strange feeling, hating Aric for what he'd done, but at the same time understanding his decision.

She was safe from the vampires, but was she safe from herself? "What if I bite someone?"

Aaron dragged her hand to his lips and let his kiss linger on his knuckles. "It's been a week, and you can't hide up in Harper's Mountains forever. It's time to get back to your life, Alana. You can't be afraid of your bear. You've shifted three times, and never once did you lose your head. Never once did you lose control. You're good at this." The smile that stretched his lips was so proud.

Alana pulled the pink winter hat farther down her ears and shook her leg in quick succession nervously as they passed the *Welcome to Bryson City* sign. Lissa had been traveling all the way from Asheville every day since Alana had been Turned to keep the café running smoothly, but Aaron was right. She needed to find some kind of normalcy. With every day she spent in the sanctuary of Harper's Mountains, she'd grown more apprehensive of messing up in the real world.

Today was huge for her. It was her first day back at the café, and she was different now. She could see and hear everything. She had all these new instincts to sort through and was easily distracted by the happenings around her.

"We have a plan. You want to repeat it?" Aaron asked.

And just like that, she settled. "I'll open the café,

get to cooking, and you'll be there to help for an hour before you have to go on shift at the firehouse."

"Yep. And what about after work?"

"I'll walk down to the fire station to visit you and get the truck keys. Harper will meet me there, and she's going with me to the courthouse to register with the Bloodrunner Crew."

Aaron's smile turned megawatt at that part. "And what will you put in the space about your mate?"

"Your name. Aaron Keller, grizzly shifter, Bloodrunner Crew." And now it was her turn to kiss his hand because she still couldn't believe she got to keep him.

"And then?"

"And then I'm grabbing dinner with Harper to celebrate. And because I really think she needs a break from all the testosterone. You boys are ridiculous."

Aaron laughed and turned onto Main Street. "And then?"

She sighed. "And then I'll take your truck back home."

"Home," he murmured in a soft tone that made her glance over at him so she could see the tender look in his eyes. He wore a dark gray winter hat and his fire department shirt under his jacket. His jaw was clean-shaven for work, and his profile masculine and strong. Alana unbuckled and slid over to the middle of the bench seat right next to him, then clicked the new buckle into place. And when Aaron draped his arm over her shoulders, she rested her cheek against him.

"You're my favorite thing about my life," she said.

He kissed her hairline and murmured, "Look there."

Squinting into the early morning light, she leaned forward and stared in shock at the sign in front of her coffee shop. The old one was nowhere to be seen but had been replaced by a big, hand-carved sign stained in a deep walnut color. *Alana's Coffee & Sweets*.

Her mouth fell open when she saw the parking lot. All the trucks there were familiar, and the Bloodrunners stood out in the cold in front of her café.

Aaron parked at the end, pushed the door open, and then helped her out on his side.

"What are you all doing here?" she asked in shock. "I thought you were back in the mountains still asleep."

"Do you like your sign?" Weston asked, a slight smile curving his lips.

She looked at it again, admiring the craftsmanship. "Did you all do this?"

"The sign?" Ryder asked. "Hell no, I don't do splinters. That was Weston's part of the gift."

"Gift for what?"

Aaron pulled her against his side. "Your welcome-to-the-crew gift."

"Come on Scarey Beary," Ryder said, pushing the door to her café open.

When he flipped on the lights, Alana gasped. The windows were new and clean, and there was an antique white chandelier hanging in the center of her café.

Aaron held her hand and led her inside as the others followed directly.

Her boots creaked onto the refurbished wooden floors. There were brightly colored tables with outlets for computers, and the walls were an olive green. There was a bar with four blue stools, and wooden shelves hung behind the counter. They were decorated artistically with hand-thrown mugs and clear jars of coffee beans. Her old chalkboard had been removed, and now there were four new ones in its place. Lissa's handwriting was all over them in pink, yellow, and blue chalk.

Along the side wall was an abstract mural that looked like an interpretation of 1010 and Harper's Mountains. There was even a tiny picture of a waving mouse in the corner.

Alana spun in a slow circle and pressed her gloved hands over her cheeks to soak up the tears there. "This is even better than what I'd dreamed for this place. You all did this for me?"

"We've been coming down here all week to get work in," Harper explained. "Aaron told us your ideas, and we all pitched in. Your sister was running the shop and staying late to help every day. You..." Harpers voice shook and failed. Blinking hard, she tried again. "You are very loved."

Alana lost it, shoulders shaking, face crumpling as she let Aaron pull her against him. Harper was right. It took an act of love for a group of people to give her a gift like this—one that took this much time and thought.

"I love you guys, too. Thank you," she whispered.

Weston pulled her in and hugged her, and then Harper and Wyatt followed. When Ryder hugged her close for too long, Aaron shoved him in the head and told him to, "Piss off, bird."

And just like that, the emotional charge lessened amid the laughter.

Alana could breathe again and truly take in this moment as her crew dragged tables together into the center of the room. They chattered and bantered, and Weston grabbed a towering plate of pastries Lissa must've made. He settled them in the center of the tables, and everything was chaos as hands scrambled for the food. The chandelier threw sparkles all around the room. Wyatt roughed up Ryder's hair as the owl shifter shoved an entire strawberry pastry into his mouth. Harper was giving one of those beautiful belly laughs at something Weston said.

"Are you happy?" Aaron asked from beside her, a smile in his voice. She was the one who usually started the are-you-happy game.

Alana wrapped her arms around his waist and rested her cheek against his steady heartbeat.

Dragging her gaze from her lively crew up to her mate's clear, adoring eyes, she played their game. "You already know the answer to that."

Aaron leaned down and, coveting her, kissed her lips gently. After he eased back, he repeated the words she usually said. "I like to hear you say it."

Her chest swelled with an overwhelming joy and sense of belonging as the waves of laughter ebbed and flowed through her café.

Alana smiled up at him and whispered, "I've never been so happy."

# Want more of these characters?

Bloodrunner Bear is the second book in a five book series based in Harper's Mountains.

Check out these other books from T. S. Joyce.

**Bloodrunner Dragon**
(Harper's Mountains, Book 1)

**Air Ryder**
(Harper's Mountains, Book 3)

**Novak Raven**
(Harper's Mountains, Book 4)

**Blackwing Dragon**
(Harper's Mountains, Book 5)

# About the Author

T.S. Joyce is devoted to bringing hot shifter romances to readers. Hungry alpha males are her calling card, and the wilder the men, the more she'll make them pour their hearts out. She werebear swears there'll be no swooning heroines in her books. It takes tough-as-nails women to handle her shifters.

Experienced at handling an alpha male of her own, she lives in a tiny town, outside of a tiny city, and devotes her life to writing big stories. Foodie, wolf whisperer, ninja, thief of tiny bottles of awesome smelling hotel shampoo, nap connoisseur, movie fanatic, and zombie slayer, and most of this bio is true.

Bear Shifters? Check

Smoldering Alpha Hotness? Double Check

Sexy Scenes? Fasten up your girdles, ladies and gents, it's gonna to be a wild ride.

For more information on T. S. Joyce's work,
visit her website at
www.tsjoyce.com

Made in the USA
San Bernardino, CA
12 July 2017